"Marry me," Cody said.

"For little Sara's sake," Lauren pointed out sadly.

Then Cody said the words that made everything all right. "Not just for my daughter. For me, too."

As his lips came down on hers, Lauren had no doubt that Cody *wanted* to kiss her. It was not a duty kiss. It was demanding and possessive, and everything she wanted from him. It took her to a place where dreams could come true, and she could believe their marriage would succeed.

In Cody's arms she became a real woman, one who wanted to learn every intimate secret he had to teach....

"I want you, Lauren," he breathed.

She didn't doubt his words or the desire in his eyes. Maybe everything was going to be all right.

Maybe, in time, her husband would come to love her...the way she loved him.

W9-AFG-353

Dear Reader,

Although the anniversary is over, Silhouette Romance is still celebrating our coming of age—we'll soon be twenty-one! Be sure to join us each and every month for six emotional stories about the romantic journey from first time to forever.

And this month we've got a special Valentine's treat for you! Three stories deal with the special holiday for true lovers. Karen Rose Smith gives us a man who asks an old friend to *Be My Bride?* Teresa Southwick's latest title, *Secret Ingredient: Love,* brings back the delightful Marchetti family. And Carla Cassidy's *Just One Kiss* shows how a confirmed bachelor is brought to his knees by a special woman.

Amusing, emotional and oh-so-captivating Carolyn Zane is at it again! Her latest BRUBAKER BRIDES story, *Tex's Exasperating Heiress,* features a determined groom, a captivating heiress and the pig that brought them together. And popular author Arlene James tells of *The Mesmerizing Mr. Carlyle,* part of our AN OLDER MAN thematic miniseries. Readers will love the overwhelming attraction between this couple! Finally, *The Runaway Princess* marks Patricia Forsythe's debut in the Romance line. But Patricia is no stranger to love stories, having written many as Patricia Knoll!

Next month, look for appealing stories by Raye Morgan, Susan Meier, Valerie Parv and other exciting authors. And be sure to return in March for a new installment of the popular ROYALLY WED tales!

Happy reading!

Mary-Theresa Hussey

Mary-Theresa Hussey
Senior Editor

Please address questions and book requests to:
Silhouette Reader Service
U.S.: 3010 Walden Ave., P.O. Box 1325, Buffalo, NY 14269
Canadian: P.O. Box 609, Fort Erie, Ont. L2A 5X3

Be My Bride?

KAREN ROSE SMITH

SILHOUETTE *Romance*

Published by Silhouette Books

America's Publisher of Contemporary Romance

To Judy Miller—
for introducing me to a pastime that has brought me
countless smiles and renewed friendship. Thank you.

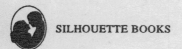 SILHOUETTE BOOKS

ISBN 0-373-19492-7

BE MY BRIDE?

Copyright © 2001 by Karen Rose Smith

This edition published by arrangement with Harlequin Books S.A.

® and TM are trademarks of Harlequin Books S.A., used under license.
Trademarks indicated with ® are registered in the United States Patent
and Trademark Office, the Canadian Trade Marks Office and in other
countries.

Visit Silhouette at www.eHarlequin.com

Printed in U.S.A.

Books by Karen Rose Smith

Silhouette Romance

*Adam's Vow #1075
*Always Daddy #1102
*Shane's Bride #1128
†Cowboy at the Wedding #1171
†Most Eligible Dad #1174
†A Groom and a Promise #1181
The Dad Who Saved
   Christmas #1267
‡Wealth, Power and a
   Proper Wife #1320
‡ Love, Honor and a
   Pregnant Bride #1326
‡Promises, Pumpkins and
   Prince Charming #1332
The Night Before Baby #1348
‡Wishes, Waltzes and a Storybook
   Wedding #1407
Just the Man She Needed #1434
Just the Husband She Chose #1455
Her Honor-Bound Lawman #1480
Be My Bride? #1492

Silhouette Special Edition

Abigail and Mistletoe #930
The Sheriff's Proposal #1074

Silhouette Books

Fortunes of Texas
Marry in Haste...

*Darling Daddies
†The Best Men
‡ Do You Take This Stranger?

Previously published under the pseudonym Kari Sutherland

Silhouette Romance

Heartfire, Homefire #973

Silhouette Special Edition

Wish on the Moon #741

KAREN ROSE SMITH

lives in Pennsylvania with her husband of twenty-nine
years. She believes in happily-ever-afters and enjoys writ-
ing about them. A former teacher, she now writes romances
full-time. She likes to hear from readers, and they can write
to her at: P.O. Box 1545, Hanover, PA 17331.

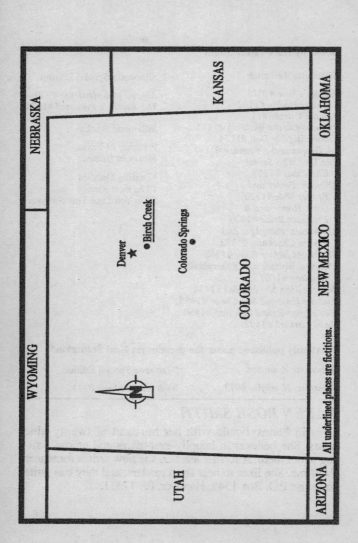

NEBRASKA

WYOMING

KANSAS

★ Denver
● Birch Creek

Colorado Springs ●

COLORADO

OKLAHOMA

UTAH

ARIZONA

NEW MEXICO

All underlined places are fictitious.

Chapter One

The doorbell rang and Lauren MacMillan's heart raced as she glanced at the two four-year-olds sitting at a miniature table. Her niece, Lindsey, was pouring imaginary tea. But it was the little girl seated at the other side of the table, tipping a small cup to a teddy bear's mouth, who captured Lauren's gaze. Sara was Cody Granger's daughter.

Cody Granger.

A memory, a regret, a humiliation that Lauren had never forgotten.

The doorbell rang again.

Sara said happily, "That's Daddy. He can have tea, too."

The last thing in the world that Lauren wanted was to invite Cody Granger to a tea party!

Turning away from Sara with her curly black hair and startling blue eyes that were just like her father's, Lauren braced herself against seeing Cody. Up until now she'd managed to avoid him since he'd moved back to Birch Creek, Colorado, a few months ago. Making herself cross the room to the foyer, she opened the door.

The cold February air blew in with a few flurries of snow, and she stared into intense blue eyes that could still take her breath away.

Dr. Cody Granger's smile vanished as he saw *her* rather than her sister-in-law, Kim. "Lauren. It's been a long time."

Cody's black wavy hair, his broad shoulders in his overcoat, his handsome face with its well-defined jaw—made Lauren's mouth go dry for a moment. Then she reminded herself she wasn't in high school any longer. "Yes, it has. Please come in," she said as if seeing him again didn't make her heart pound and bring back memories she'd rather forget. "Sara and Lindsey are playing in the family room. I took over for Kim this afternoon. She's not feeling well, and she asked me to help out."

As Lauren closed the door behind Cody, she caught a tantalizing trace of his spicy aftershave. Instead of heading for the family room, he turned to look at her again. His unreadable gaze held hers long enough to completely unnerve her.

"Sara and Lindsey are having a tea party," she murmured inanely as she broke eye contact and went into the family room.

"What's wrong with Kim?" Cody asked, coming up beside her in two long strides. He sounded concerned.

"She's nauseous and terribly dizzy. I have her settled upstairs with soda and crackers."

When Cody's daughter saw him, she smiled at her

father brightly. "Hi, Daddy. We're having tea. Want some?"

Crouching beside her, Cody gave his daughter a hug. "I think I'll pass on the tea. Did you have a good day today?"

Sara nodded as she told him all about it. "Lauren played with us. We drew pictures and after Matt went to bed, we played Candyland.

Cody chuckled. "You *did* have a busy day."

Redheaded Lindsey piped up, "Mommy's not feeling so good."

"That's what Lauren tells me." Cody straightened. "Why don't I check on Kim while I'm here? My bag's in the car."

Apparently considering the question rhetorical, he was almost across the room before Lauren could say, "Cody, wait. Maybe Kim doesn't want you to look in on her."

His gaze held hers as his brows arched. "Why wouldn't she? If it's nothing serious, I can give her something to help the symptoms."

He was right, and Lauren didn't know why she was objecting. Probably because she didn't want his help or to be indebted to him or have him hanging around any longer than necessary. But she had to think about Kim's well-being.

More color gathered in her cheeks as Cody's inscrutable blue eyes seemed to examine every aspect of her appearance. She had her light-brown hair tied back in a ponytail for convenience's sake. When Kim's call had come in, she'd been working at her parents' garden center, and she'd rushed straight over. She was more slender now than when she'd known Cody in high school, and as his gaze passed over her, she felt self-conscious in her pink sweater and blue jeans.

"I guess it would be good if you had a look at her," Lauren finally capitulated. "I'll go tell her you're coming up."

She could sense his eyes still on her as she went to the stairs, feeling sixteen again. The memories she'd pushed into the past seemed as if they'd happened only yesterday. As much as she'd tried to deny it since she'd heard Cody Granger had returned to Birch Creek, the hurt he'd caused her so long ago was still alive in her heart.

Why couldn't she forget a teenage infatuation? Why couldn't she forget that first reaching for a dream? Because the way Cody had crushed it had affected her more deeply than she'd ever wanted to admit.

With determination that had grown stronger over the years, she climbed the steps with her back straight and her chin high. In a few minutes Cody Granger would be out of her life again, and everything would return to normal.

Fifteen minutes later Cody folded his stethoscope and stuffed it into his black leather bag. Lauren had hovered while he'd examined her sister-in-law. Then she'd left the room a few moments after he'd diagnosed Kim with a virus that had been going around for the past couple of weeks, murmuring that she had to check on Matt and keep her eye on the girls. Cody was grateful she was conscientious, but he had the feeling she'd left quickly to avoid him.

After he took packets of tablets from his bag, he

said, "Take one every four hours for the dizziness. They should help."

Closing his bag, he looked over at Kim who was propped against pillows in the bed. She was pale and her freckles stood out more than they usually did. Her red hair against the white pillow case was a splash of color.

She looked so morose, he said, "You *will* feel better in a couple of days."

"I want to feel better *now*."

He chuckled and shook his head. When he'd returned to Birch Creek and needed a sitter for Sara while he worked, Eli Hastings—his longtime mentor and now partner in a family medical practice—had suggested Kim because she'd lived right up the street from Cody's new home. She'd baby-sat for Eli's granddaughter whenever his daughter was in a pinch.

Kim was a caring young woman, around Cody's own age of thirty-one, and she was usually full of energy. The unhappy expression on her face told him she wanted to be on the move, rather than in bed. "Just think of the next few days as enforced relaxation," he suggested.

She gave him a wry smile. "When I relax, I like to do it with Rob, preferably on the ski slopes." After taking a tiny sip of her soda, Kim lay back on the pillows, eyeing Cody for a moment. "What's with you and Lauren?"

"I'm not sure what you mean." From the warm and friendly way Kim had acted since he'd met her, he suspected she knew nothing about his history with her sister-in-law, though her husband Rob probably did.

"Lauren's quiet," Kim mused. "But she's usually...friendly. I could almost feel frost in the air while she was in here.''

''We knew each other in high school,'' he said as casually as he could, and picked up his bag.

''Knew?''

For years he'd regretted what had happened with Lauren. ''If you want details, you should ask Lauren. Are you still dizzy?''

''I'm fine as long as I don't move my head. And not too dizzy to realize you changed the subject.''

''That's because I'm going to leave, and you're going to rest. That's what's best for you now.''

She sighed. ''So you say. You don't have to worry about getting another sitter tomorrow. Lauren said she'll watch the kids.''

Maybe Lauren would baby-sit Kim's children, but he didn't know if she'd want to watch Sara again. Crossing to the door, he said, ''I'll firm things up with her. Take it easy and call me if your fever spikes.''

Kim nodded, then frowned as if the movement made her dizzy again.

Gently closing the bedroom door, Cody heard the sounds of Lindsey's and Sara's laughter as he stepped into the hallway. Descending the steps, he realized the girls' voices were coming from the kitchen.

Leaving his bag in the foyer where he'd laid his coat, he saw Sara and Lindsey were seated in the corner on the linoleum, building towers with blocks. Lauren stood at the kitchen counter, holding two-and-a-half-year-old Matt in one arm while she tried to tear lettuce leaves one-handed.

''It's a little tough to make supper with an armful.'' More than anything, Cody wanted to get on a friendly footing with Lauren and put the past behind them.

She hitched Matt higher on her hip, her gaze quickly passing over Cody's white dress shirt and tie. Then she concentrated on what she was doing again. ''Sometimes he's grouchy when he wakes up. He just wants me to hold him. But Rob's going to be home anytime, and I wanted to have supper well on the way.''

Seeing Cody, Matt held his arms out to him.

With a grin Cody took the little boy from Lauren. ''Hey, partner. What's up? Did you have a good nap?''

Matt nodded and laid his head against Cody's shoulder, sticking his thumb into his mouth.

''He doesn't go to just anyone like that,'' Lauren said, sounding surprised.

''Matt and I are old pals. Sometimes he feels outnumbered. If I arrive before Rob gets home, it kind of evens up the score.''

After a brief silence, Lauren cleared her throat. ''I see.''

He should have chosen another set of words. The tension humming between him and Lauren increased as he couldn't keep from looking at her. She'd become a beautiful woman, so different from the slightly overweight teenager who'd cared more about her studies than the current styles. She hadn't been the type of girl who'd stood out. Not like Gretchen DeWitt. But Lauren had had a smile that lit up her brown eyes, as well as long, light-brown hair that shone with gold when she stood in the sun. He'd been so head-over-heels involved with Gretchen back then, he hadn't much looked at other girls.

Not until he and Gretchen had broken up. Not until Lauren had interviewed him for the article in the school newspaper. Not until he'd asked her to his senior prom.

Breaking eye contact, Lauren busied herself with the salad fixings at the counter. "I'll be taking care of Matt and Lindsey here tomorrow. If you want to drop Sara off in the morning as you usually do, that's fine."

Coming up behind her, wishing she would face him again, he asked, "You're sure?"

"Absolutely," she said briskly.

He clasped her elbow. "Lauren..."

She did face him then, and he was all too aware of his fingers on her soft skin, but most of all the defiant look in her dark-brown eyes as she pulled out of his grasp and stepped a good two feet away. "I really do have to fix supper, Cody." Then she moved to the table and picked up a few papers. "These are Sara's drawings that she wanted to take along."

After Lauren handed them to him, she took Matt from his arms and cuddled him close.

If she didn't want to have a conversation with him, so be it. His spare time was limited, and he had a stack of medical journals to read tonight after he put Sara to bed. "I usually drop Sara off around seven-thirty."

"That's fine." Lauren still avoided his gaze and smoothed back Matt's hair.

Cody knew he had no right to feel annoyed with Lauren's attitude. They'd never discussed what had happened between them that afternoon a few days before the prom. After that day they hadn't spoken again. From Lauren's attitude they weren't going to talk now, either.

All of Cody's life he'd learned that if he didn't move forward he'd get sucked back. Eli Hastings had made moving forward possible for him, and he knew better than to look back. He knew he couldn't undo the past. He'd risen above his father's past and he'd risen above his own. Now he had a daughter to raise and a practice to concentrate on. If Lauren MacMillan didn't want to be friends, he could live with that.

Going to the corner of the kitchen, he held his hand out to his daughter. Sara scrambled to her feet and took it, giving him a huge smile. She was his life now, and he didn't need anyone else.

"Thanks for checking on Kim," Lauren said politely.

"Anytime. I'll see you in the morning," he said to Lauren.

Conversation came to an abrupt standstill again, and he went into the foyer to retrieve his coat and Sara's, as well as his bag.

Minutes later, as he and Sara left Rob and Kim MacMillan's house, Cody tried to put Lauren's face out of his head.

He couldn't.

But he told himself he would.

After dinner with Rob and the kids, Lauren had made sure her brother had everything under control and that Kim was resting comfortably. Then she'd returned to her apartment on the other side of town. She had work to do on a design for gardens she was submitting to a firm in Denver that was putting up a new office complex. If she could win this assignment, there would be others like it, helping not only her career as a landscape architect but her parents' garden center as well. Yet as she leafed through catalogs she'd spread across her kitchen table, she couldn't help but think about Cody Granger.

After medical school he'd completed his residency in Colorado Springs and set up practice there. Kim had told Lauren that his wife, Gretchen, had died two years ago. Lauren didn't know any of the details and reminded herself she didn't want to know any of them. Yet she couldn't help feeling compassion for Sara who had to grow up without a mother. Lauren couldn't imagine her own mother not being around. Where her father and Rob had always been protective, Verna MacMillan had been a steady support throughout Lauren's life.

Still, when her mother had suggested she move home after she'd earned her degree in landscape architecture, Lauren had known she needed her independence. She'd needed to build on the confidence her successes in college had given her.

She'd been shy in grade school and no one had paid much attention to her. That had been okay with her. But when other girls her age had started blooming, she'd gained weight—not a lot, yet enough to make her feel different…enough to make her realize that boys liked the thin, sexy girls. Her mother had forbidden her to diet, insisting instead she simply eat healthily and eventually she would come into her own.

Lauren had never known what that meant, not until her freshman year at college when the extra weight had melted away…when she'd found a hairstyle that had complemented her features...when she'd found out how much she enjoyed the career she'd chosen. She loved her family dearly and liked working with them at the garden center every day, but she needed her own life, too, separate from them.

Building her career would ensure her independence.

She began searching the catalogs in earnest, hoping something she came across would spark a unique idea for the office complex's courtyard.

When her phone rang, it startled her, and she worried that Kim might be feeling worse.

But after she greeted the caller, she heard Cody Granger's voice.

"Lauren, it's Cody. I'm on call tonight and I just got paged. Usually Kim can baby-sit for me at the drop of a hat. I tried another sitter I sometimes use, but she's not home. Would it be possible for you to come over to my house? Sara's ready for bed. If that's too much of an imposition, I can bring her to you. But I don't know how late I'll be."

She told herself she could say no. She told herself Cody Granger's problem wasn't hers. Yet when she thought of little Sara, she knew she couldn't refuse him. "I can be there in ten minutes."

"I really appreciate this, Lauren. I'll pay you, of course—"

"Don't be ridiculous. I'll bring work along. I can design as easily at your house as I can here."

"Thanks, Lauren."

She didn't want his thanks, and yet she didn't know what she *did* want from him.

When Lauren parked in the snow-lined driveway of Cody's house, she reminded herself again she was only doing this for Sara's sake. And as she walked up the cleared front path, she willed her heart rate to slow and grasped her briefcase just a little tighter. She'd passed Cody's house many times, but she'd never been inside. She'd also tried not to wonder what kind of man the star quarterback of the Birch Creek Crusaders had become.

The house was an attractive two-story with a covered front porch and a double garage, part brick and part beige siding. She had to smile as she stepped onto the porch, because there was one adult-size sled there, as well as a matching child-size one. From Sara's behavior as well as comments that Kim had made, Lauren guessed Cody was a good father...a loving father.

When he opened the door, his face was serious as he motioned her inside.

Lauren was careful not to get too close to him. He was wearing a sweatshirt, jeans and black boots. The casual dress emphasized the mature muscled fitness of his body rather than the leaner physique of his youth. He'd always exuded virile appeal.

Stepping farther away from that appeal, she took off her blue parka and went to the sofa where Sara was sitting, a book on her lap. "Hi, honey. Did your daddy tell you I'm going to put you to bed and stay until he comes home?"

With an engaging smile, Sara handed her a book. "Read this?"

Cody went to his daughter, too, and gave her a big hug. "One story, then bed. It's already past your bedtime. I'll see you in the morning."

"'Night, Daddy."

Cody gave Lauren a wry grin. "She's used to this.

Sometimes I get the feeling she's happy to have someone else put her to bed.''

Lauren heard the concern underlying his amusement, and she realized being a single parent had to be very difficult. "We'll read a story, and then I'll tuck her in.''

Taking a card from his pocket, he handed it to her. "I've got to get going. This is my pager number. If you need me, call.''

Lauren nodded.

Their eyes locked for a few long seconds, and everything in the room seemed to go absolutely still. But then Cody grabbed a black leather bomber jacket from the back of a chair and headed for the door. After a wave he closed it behind him.

Lauren tucked his card into her pocket, then sat on the sofa and smiled at Sara. The four-year-old took that as an invitation and scooted closer to Lauren, nestling at her side. When Lauren opened the book, she put her arm around Sara, and a deep yearning ached in her heart. She wanted to be a mother, and maybe she hadn't realized how much until this moment. As many times as she'd played with and held and bathed Kim's children, motherhood had been a far-off dream. But tonight, sitting here with Sara, feeling her warm little body cuddled close, it became more than a dream. It became a need.

After Lauren read Sara's book, Sara asked for a glass of milk, and Lauren knew she was stalling. But she let her and went to the kitchen. Cody's house was comfortable and beautifully furnished. The teal-and-tan decor of the living room and the gleaming oak wood was complemented by various tones of the two shades in the dining room draperies. Four oak chairs were positioned around a rectangular table. But the hutch against one wall was empty.

Lauren glanced into the solarium off the dining room and saw a few lawn chairs. Otherwise it, too, was bare.

While she poured Sara a glass of milk in the kitchen, the little girl crawled up onto a high-backed stool at the eat-in counter and kept up a running conversation about anything and everything.

But finally it was time for bed, and Sara didn't stall any longer. When she led Lauren to her bedroom, Lauren could see that the four-year-old's room was as sparse-looking as the dining room. There was a single bed with an oak headboard, a chest and a small dresser. The walls were white, and no curtains hung at the window, just a miniblind. A pink blanket covered white sheets on the bed. Lauren thought about what she'd do to the room to liven it up, to make it a little girl's haven.

She spotted a five-by-seven picture sitting on the dresser. Gretchen had been even more beautiful in her twenties than she'd been at eighteen, with her blond, curly hair and big blue eyes. Cody's high school sweetheart. Lauren had been so foolish to think she could ever begin to compete with a cheerleader whose beauty outshone every other girl's in the school.

Had Cody dated since his wife died? Certainly a man like him wouldn't want to be without a woman in his bed for long. Unbidden, Lauren remembered his kisses. That one night, when kissing had turned to touching....

Sara scrambled into bed and asked, ''Can you

leave the hall light on? Daddy turns it off when he comes home.''

It was probably a signal between them. If Sara woke up in the middle of the night and the hall light was off, she knew her father had returned.

"Sure, I'll leave it on. And I'll be just downstairs in the living room. I'll leave your door open, and if you need anything you just call me, okay?'' She pulled the covers up to Sara's chin.

Sara looked up at her. "You can kiss me goodnight. Daddy always does.''

Lauren smiled and leaned over, placing a tender kiss on the little girl's forehead.

When she returned downstairs, she opened her briefcase and took out her legal pad and a few catalogs. If she immersed herself in her work, the time would pass quickly. If she immersed herself in her work, she would forget she was in Cody Granger's house.

It was almost midnight when Lauren heard the sound of Cody's SUV in the driveway. The garage door went up, and a few moments later she heard him in the kitchen. She'd been reclining on the sofa, propped against the arm with her work on her lap. Hearing the sound of his footsteps, she swung her legs over the side and sat up straight.

When he appeared in the living room, she took a deep breath. He'd apparently left his jacket in the kitchen. He was all-male—tall, muscular, strong. And when he came over and sat beside her on the couch, she was more aware of her attraction to him than she'd ever been.

"How'd it go?'' he asked. He looked tired, and she imagined his day had been even longer than hers.

"Just fine. Sarah's been asleep since I put her to bed. I looked in on her twice. How about you? Is the emergency past?"

"For now," he said, his voice deep. "It's one of my elderly patients with heart problems. He's been hospitalized twice in the past three months. His lungs filled with fluid again. We got him turned around, but..." Cody's voice dropped lower. "It's just a matter of time."

Lauren could see the pain in Cody's eyes and the compassion that he obviously felt for his patients. "How do you handle it?" she asked.

When his gaze met hers, she could see he understood what she meant. "There are as many good days as there are rough ones, thank goodness. Most of the time, I can help my patients, or at least make them more comfortable. But when all of it really gets to me—" he paused for a moment "—I take out my bike and ride like the wind."

"Your bike?"

His smile was crookedly boyish. "Yep. I bought a motorcycle last year, and it was the best investment I've ever made. I use it for quick trips around town and on the paths down by the creek. Now and then I take it on the interstate. Have you ever ridden one?"

There had always been a wild side to Cody. When she'd interviewed him so long ago for the school paper, he'd admitted to her he'd been down to the police station a couple of times. He'd also revealed that if it hadn't been for Eli Hastings, he wouldn't have made the football team or improved his grades or applied for college scholarships. Lauren had heard rumors about Cody's father, but she'd had such a crush on Cody that nothing had mattered except the moments she'd spent with him.

"I've never even thought about riding a motorcycle," she said now.

His blue eyes filled with amusement at the tone of her voice. "From the sound of it, you classify it with jumping off a diving tower or tightrope walking. It's really much saner than either of those."

She couldn't keep the blush from her cheeks. As she had so many years ago, she felt inexperienced and awkward in his presence. "I guess it depends on your point of view."

His eyes hadn't left her face, and she felt a compelling urge to lean closer to him. He must have felt it, too, because he leaned closer to her. "I'll take you on a ride sometime...if you'd like." His voice was slow and deep and resonated through her.

Riding on a motorcycle behind Cody, her arms wrapped around his waist...

Maybe one of them moved or both of them moved or the space between them just seemed to vanish. His shoulder brushed hers.

She raised her chin.

He bent his head.

All evening Cody had thought about Lauren. She was so sweet, with an air of innocence still surrounding her. How many men had she dated? How many men had she kissed? How many men had she been with since that night in his car when she'd told him he was the first boy to ever touch her. He'd wanted her back then, but he'd put the brakes on his desire. He'd been older and experienced enough to know that Lauren was the type of girl who saved herself for the right man. His feelings had still been in an upheaval about his breakup with Gretchen. Probably the most noble thing he'd ever done was not to take advantage of Lauren that night.

And now...?

The last thing he wanted was a relationship. His marriage had been a disappointment that was still a puzzle. Above all, he'd learned loving caused heartache and frustration. He didn't want any part of it—except for loving his daughter.

Straightening, he got a grip on the adrenaline rushing through him and stood. "Are you sure I can't pay you for your time tonight?"

For a moment there was a flare of emotion in Lauren's eyes. But then it disappeared into a cool guardedness. "Putting Sara to bed was a joy. I don't need to be paid."

Breaking eye contact, she scooped the catalogs from the sofa and pushed them into her briefcase on the coffee table. Then she added the legal pad and pen and snapped the lid shut.

"I'll walk you to your car," he offered, unsettled by a desire he hadn't felt since long before Gretchen died.

"That's not necessary." Picking up her briefcase, she quickly crossed to the door. "I'll see you in the morning."

He nodded.

As Lauren walked down the path to the driveway, he watched her. He shouldn't have even *thought* about kissing her. What had gotten into him?

She backed out of his driveway, and as her taillights faded into the distance, he shut his front door and locked it with a firm click. Whatever had gotten into him, wouldn't again. He knew better than to tempt fate a second time.

Chapter Two

The following day Cody dropped Sara off at Kim's in the morning, and Lauren was coolly polite. He was, as well, telling himself that was best, though he couldn't help but notice the way the waves of her hair brushed her cheeks, the way her lavender sweater molded to her breasts. In the evening when he stopped to pick up Sara, he only exchanged a few words with Lauren.

But at eight that night she phoned him. When he heard her voice he was surprised. "Is something wrong?" Maybe she'd decided baby-sitting wasn't her cup of tea...or rather baby-sitting *his* daughter wasn't.

"Kim's feeling better," Lauren explained. "But Lindsey's not feeling well now. Kim doesn't think you should bring Sara over tomorrow. Do you have anyone else who can watch her?"

He heard the hopeful note in her voice that he did. But he couldn't tell her what she wanted to hear. "I don't. Not on short notice like this. I can look into a day-care center, but I have to be at the hospital early tomorrow. One of my patients is having surgery.''

There was a lengthy pause. ''Kim suggested I take care of Sara at your house.''

He could hear Lauren's uncertainty, and he didn't expect her to do him any favors. Maybe he could find an off-duty nurse— ''I've imposed on you enough.'' Lauren had her own career, her own life.

''I'm thinking about Sara, Cody. I hate to see her thrust into a strange situation when she doesn't have to be. If you'd like me to watch her tomorrow, I will.''

Remembering how happy his daughter had been in Lauren's care, knowing how important that was, he asked, ''You're sure?''

''Yes, I'm sure,'' she answered softly.

''I'll make some calls tomorrow. I obviously need to find someone as a backup for Kim. Can you be here by seven-thirty?''

''I'll be there. Good night.''

''Good night.'' He thought about other good nights, the chaste kiss he'd given Lauren on their first date, the more passionate kisses on their second and third dates. At the click of the receiver as Lauren hung up, he found himself looking forward to morning.

Sara was delighted the following morning when she found out Lauren would be coming over. Cody left the house as Lauren was scrambling eggs for his daughter. The good smells coming from the kitchen made him wish he was staying and eating breakfast with them. Usually he simply gave Sara cereal for breakfast. He knew they relied too much on take-out and fast food, especially pizza. But they managed.

That evening, though, Sara ran to him as he came in the door. "Can Lauren stay for supper with us? Please?"

He lifted the bag in his arms. "It just so happens I brought Chinese. There's always enough for one or two more." Seeing the uncertain expression on Lauren's face, he gave her an out. "Unless you want to get home."

But Sara obviously didn't even want to consider her new sitter and friend going home as she tugged on Lauren's hand. "Stay for supper. Pl-e-ease. Daddy has funny sticks to eat the noodles with."

Cody waited for Lauren's answer.

When she looked up at him, he added, "We'd both like you to stay."

Breaking eye contact, Lauren gazed down at his daughter. "If I stay, will you show me how to use the wooden sticks?"

Sara nodded vigorously. "I don't do it good, but Daddy does. He can show you. Come on." Tugging Lauren by the hand, Sara led her into the kitchen.

While Sara told Cody everything she'd done with Lauren that day, he took dishes from the cupboard and chopsticks from a drawer. When he sat beside Lauren at the round, oak kitchen table, his knee brushed hers. But she moved away, and he was sorry she had.

He opened the sweet-and-sour chicken while she opened the chicken lo mein. "Did you talk to Kim today?" he asked.

Using the fork, Lauren dumped the container of lo

mein into a serving dish so they'd all have access to it. "She's much better, but Lindsey isn't."

"I made calls this afternoon," he said. "But I didn't have much luck. The day-care center's full until they get more help. One of the women a patient recommended is out of town. There was another, but I'd want to interview her before I'd let her take care of Sara." From his marriage to Gretchen he'd learned caretaking of a child was a gift that some women weren't born with. But he could see Lauren truly liked being with Sara. "I know you have your own work to do, but I'll pay you handsomely to finish out the rest of the week. I won't leave Sara with someone I don't know if I can trust."

Lauren was about to pour rice into another dish, but she set the container down and looked at him. "Why do you trust me?"

That was a terrifically complicated question, yet a simple one, too. "Kim trusts you with her kids. That's a sterling recommendation. And I've seen you with Sara. She's the best judge."

Before Lauren could respond, the telephone rang.

Pushing his chair back, he went to the counter and picked up the cordless phone. "Grangers'," he said, as he watched Sara pick up the chopsticks and try to show Lauren how to use them.

"Cody, it's Dolores," a woman's voice said. "Do you have a few minutes?"

Cody's gaze settled on his daughter. Dolores DeWitt, Gretchen's mother, had not approved of his move back to Birch Creek with Sara. She'd wanted him to stay in Colorado Springs where she could see Sara more often. But he'd had his reasons for wanting to move away from Dolores's influence. He didn't want Sara growing up as spoiled and selfish as he'd finally discovered Gretchen had been.

"We're just sitting down to supper," he told her.

"Then I won't keep you long. I want you to bring Sara for a visit. Let her stay with me, maybe for a week."

Cody looked over at Sara and Lauren who were giggling as they tried to maneuver noodles into their mouths with the sticks. Something inside Cody recoiled at having Sara stay with her grandmother for that long. "This isn't a good time, Dolores."

"With your long hours I'd think you'd be glad to let me take responsibility for Sara for a little while."

A tone had crept into his mother-in-law's voice lately that bothered him. He didn't like it, as he sensed it could mean trouble.

"It's because of my long hours that I don't want Sara away from me for a week," he explained calmly. "I like to spend as much time with her as I can. But I'll tell you what. I'll look at my schedule, and we'll drive up and visit you soon."

"And *soon* means..." his mother-in-law prompted.

"It means I'll check with Eli and see what his plans are for the next couple of weekends. Then I'll get back to you."

"If you had joined one of the prestigious group practices up here—"

"But I didn't, Dolores, and I'm happy here. So is Sara."

"I *lived* in Birch Creek, Cody. I know what's there and what isn't. Colorado Springs has so much more to offer. I don't understand why you moved."

Trying to remain patient, he took a deep breath. "My roots are here."

"Roots? For most of your life you tried to escape your roots according to Gretchen. You built a life *here*. You and Gretchen had become part of the Colorado Springs community. You should see the new hospital wing. It's almost finished. Every time I pass by it, I think about the great contribution Gretchen made by helping with fund-raising for it."

Gretchen's charity work had become a sore spot between them after Sara was born. But Dolores had never seen that. She'd never seen a lot of things, because she hadn't wanted to. To keep peace, he assured her, "I'll take a tour of it when it's finished. We *will* visit soon, Dolores."

"But you won't tell me when," she said, her voice terse.

"I can't until Eli and I discuss our schedules. You're welcome to come visit here if you'd like. You know that."

"Yes, but even after all these years, I don't want to run into David or his friends."

Dolores had divorced David DeWitt and moved with her daughter to Colorado Springs after Gretchen graduated from high school. There wasn't much chance Dolores would run into her ex-husband, who was a financial advisor, if she just visited her granddaughter. But she'd used that as an excuse since Cody and Sara had returned to Birch Creek. "Whatever you decide, Dolores. Just keep in mind it might be a few weeks until I can get away from here, especially on a weekend."

"All right," she snapped. "Check your calendar. Check with your partner. But then we'll have to talk seriously about my spending more time with Sara. I'm her grandmother, after all.''

She was a grandmother who wanted everything her own way...just as Gretchen had. "I'll call you in a few days," he assured her.

After a terse goodbye, his mother-in-law hung up.

Cody took his seat again and filled his plate with rice. Then he piled sweet-and-sour chicken onto it and poured red sauce on top. His gut instinct told him something was brewing with Dolores.

"That was Gretchen's mother?" Lauren asked.

"Yes." Knowing Lauren had overheard the conversation, he added, "She tried to persuade me not to move back here."

"But you did, anyway."

His arm brushed Lauren's as he picked up a set of chopsticks, and he didn't move away. This time neither did she. "I wanted to raise Sara in a small town."

"But your mother-in-law wants you closer."

He shook his head. "It's not just that. I get the feeling she thinks she could do a better job raising Sara. And when Dolores wants something, she goes after it."

"You mean custody?" Lauren sounded shocked.

That had been the worry that had been niggling at him for a few weeks. Yet he wouldn't placate Dolores and in the process do something he didn't think was good for Sara. "I hope I'm wrong."

Not wanting to discuss in front of his daughter either his mother-in-law or a possibility he'd rather not think about, he asked Sara, "Did you teach Lauren how to use the chopsticks?"

"I tried, but I'm done now. Can I go watch cartoons?"

Glancing at his watch, he nodded. "I'll tell you when time's up."

With a grin she slid off her chair and ran to the living room.

"You limit her time watching TV?" Lauren asked.

Her wide brown eyes were curious, and he felt more drawn to her than he ever had. "I'd rather see her putting puzzles together or playing with her dolls. Once it stays light longer, we'll go outside after supper."

Studying him with the same intensity with which he was studying her, she murmured, "You're a good father, Cody."

Her words filled him with a pride he hadn't felt in a long time. They meant a lot. "Sometimes I'm not sure just how good a father I am."

Lauren tilted her head, and the overhead lighting shone on the blond strands in her hair. "Being a single parent has to be tough," she said.

Right now, he wasn't thinking of being a parent. The floral scent of Lauren's perfume, her beautiful eyes, the pink perfection of her skin, called to all his masculine instincts and aroused him. Laying down his chopsticks, he realized he'd lost his appetite for food. Another, baser appetite had taken its place.

Lauren's brown eyes grew large and wide as awareness pounded between them. The longing to kiss her was so strong it overshadowed Cody's good sense. He was aroused just by looking at her like this. It was crazy. He hadn't even thought about taking a woman to bed for such a long time. But here and now he wanted Lauren. And he wanted her to want him.

Anticipation trembled between them until he slowly slid his hand under her hair...until he urged her forward...until he bent his head to her....

But this time it was Lauren who backed away. As she jerked out of his clasp, she looked angry. Shoving back her chair, she stood. "This isn't going to work, Cody. You'll have to find someone else to take care of Sara."

He knew it was long past time they cleared the air. Rising to his feet, he said, "This doesn't have anything to do with Sara."

"No, I guess it doesn't. It has to do with my very good memory."

Beneath the anger he saw something else and suddenly realized it was pain—pain that was still there after all these years. He'd never meant to hurt her. He'd never meant for her to see him and Gretchen—

"I can't pretend we're friends, Cody," Lauren rushed on, her face flushed now. "I can't pretend we ever were." Then she turned away from him and headed for the living room.

He went after her.

But she was out the door so quickly that Sara, watching her cartoon, hadn't even noticed. He thought about stopping Lauren from leaving, but there was no way he could rewrite history. There was no way he could erase the betrayal Lauren had felt. He'd been foolish to think that the years had made a difference...that time had healed. He could see now that time hadn't made any difference at all.

The best thing that he could do for Lauren was to leave her alone.

* * *

"Daddy, how long am I gonna be here? Can I go see what Nancy's doin'?"

For at least the tenth time, Cody switched off his hand-held tape recorder. He'd had no choice but to bring Sara to the office with him today. He was trying to get caught up on patient notes. Even though his daughter was supposed to be putting puzzles together and being quiet for just a little while, her "little" while and his were definitely different. Every two minutes she asked him another question. Maybe he should just handwrite the patient notes and be done with it.

"Nancy's busy right now, honey. Would you rather color than put puzzles together?"

"Uh-huh."

He'd packed a bag with toys and supplies he'd thought Sara might need, and now he settled her with crayons and a coloring book on the floor by the window. Then he reminded himself where he'd stopped his dictation.

But his mind wasn't on patient notes. Rather, it was on Lauren. And last night. And thirteen years ago.

Remembering the day he'd broken up with Gretchen, her voice still seemed as clear as the proverbial bell. *We're going to colleges miles away from each other, Cody. I know we're going steady, but I won't see you for months, and...I want to date other guys.*

The words had come almost as a physical blow. He'd been dating Gretchen for six months and had already dreamed of their future together, even though she came from a well-to-do family and he knew that her parents didn't approve of him. But that hadn't mattered to Gretchen. She'd come up to him at a party, complimented him for the touchdowns he'd made in the homecoming game. She'd been the Homecoming Princess, and he'd been awestruck by her beauty from the moment he'd set eyes on her. She was everything an eighteen-year-old boy could want.

He'd wanted someone of his own to love all of his life. Gretchen had filled the cavernous emptiness inside of him left by a father who had been in and out of jail and a mother who'd worked long hours to provide for them. Carol Granger had worked six days a week, was tired all the time, and could never seem to get everything done, though Cody helped by working any job he could find.

When he'd found Gretchen, he thought he'd found the answer to the loneliness he'd always felt. But then that April day she'd told him he wasn't enough...she wanted to spread her wings. He should have seen the warning signs. He should have realized then that they had different goals. He'd wanted a family, roots and a respectable career. She'd wanted a lifestyle she'd been accustomed to all her life.

He'd tried to convince himself the breakup was for the best. He had a long road ahead through college and medical school. It had been hard to admit, but he'd been devastated by her lack of faith in them as a couple. He should have realized Gretchen always did what was best for her. But he'd been too blinded by her charm and beauty. He hadn't seen deeper until after they were married.

The day after his breakup with Gretchen, Lauren had approached him about the interview for the school newspaper. There had been such a sweetness about her that he'd liked being with her. She'd made his bruised ego and shattered dreams seem not quite as devastating. That's why he'd asked her to the prom. He still remembered the sparkle in her eyes and the radiance on her face...her total disbelief that he was asking *her.* They'd gone out after she'd accepted his invitation, and he'd had to rein in teenage hormones when their kissing and then their touching had gotten out of hand.

That was a week before the prom, and then a few days later...

It had been a bright, sunny May day. He'd been shooting hoops after school with a few friends when Gretchen had come up to him and asked if they could talk. They'd stepped into the shade of a maple beside the school building when Gretchen looked up at him with those shimmering blue eyes of hers....

"I made a mistake, Cody. I was wrong to want to date other guys. You're the only one I want to see, even if we are miles apart." Then she'd wrapped her arms around his neck and they'd kissed.

Cody hadn't asked why she'd changed her mind. He'd just felt as if fate had blessed his world again. Giving in to the desire he *could* satisfy with Gretchen, they'd kissed with all the teenage passion in their hearts.

And then his friend Barry called his name and penetrated his happy haze. "Heads up, Cody," his friend said.

When Cody broke the kiss and looked over Gretchen's shoulder, he saw Lauren with a group of girls. There was a stunned expression on her face, followed by pain, and he saw her chin quiver. She turned and ran, and he knew he had to go after her.

Gretchen clasped his arm as he started off. "Will I see you tonight?"

More confused than he'd ever felt, he said, "I'll call you," then hurried after Lauren.

He heard the tittering and chuckles of the other students standing around as he jogged after Lauren and finally caught up with her. "We have to talk."

But she'd pulled away from him. "We don't have anything to talk about."

She would have run off again, except he blocked her path. He was too big for her to dodge, too strong for her to escape from. As she saw that, she straightened her shoulders and lifted her chin, even though tears still glistened in her eyes. "You obviously want to go to the prom with Gretchen. I won't hold you to your invitation."

"I invited *you* to the prom. I'm going to take *you*."

She shook her head, wrapping her arms tighter around her books. "I won't be a duty date, Cody. You go back to Gretchen, and you have fun at the prom." Instead of trying to get around him, she turned to her left and crossed the street, hurrying away from him and from the embarrassment he'd caused her.

Cody had always regretted what had happened that day. He'd waited at her locker the next morning, but she'd never arrived. When he called her home, she wouldn't take his calls. Finally getting the message, he'd only caught glimpses of her in the school halls from then on. She'd avoided him, which wasn't difficult, since most seniors and sophomores didn't mingle. Two weeks after the prom he and Gretchen had graduated, eventually marrying during his first year of residency.

If he had only realized Gretchen had wanted to be a doctor's wife more than she'd wanted to be *his* wife. If he had only realized how she truly felt about having children. But they'd been miles apart before their wedding, and he'd been blinded by what he *thought* she was. All that beauty and charm hadn't gone much deeper than her achieving her next goal in life.

His daughter's voice shattered his reverie. "Can I go see Nancy now?"

"Color one more picture, then we'll see what she's doing."

"One more?"

"One more."

And while Sara was doing that, he picked up the phone, knowing he'd waited too long to set things straight with Lauren. Looking up the number for MacMillan's Garden Center, he dialed it quickly.

"MacMillan's," a soft, feminine voice answered, and he recognized Lauren immediately.

"Lauren, it's Cody."

There was silence.

"I'm sorry," he said. The words carried a vehemence that surprised even him.

After a pause she asked, "For what?"

He imagined she was thinking about the almost-kiss. "For hurting you back in high school. For not insisting on taking you to the prom. For not settling things between us before now."

After a long pause she responded, "There's nothing to settle, Cody."

"I never meant to hurt you or to embarrass you."

Sara scrambled to her feet and came running toward him. "I'm all done, Daddy. Let's go see Nancy now." She thrust a picture of a red-and-blue ball, hurriedly colored, under his nose. He encircled her with his arm.

"Are you at home?" Lauren asked.

"No, at my office."

Sara wiggled her picture in front of him. "Isn't it good, Daddy?"

He covered the mouthpiece. "It's very good, honey. Now just give me a few more minutes."

"Is Sara at your office with you?" Lauren asked, surprised.

"Yes." He didn't want her to think he'd called because of that.

Sitting at her own desk at the garden center, Lauren debated with herself. Last night when Kim had called to find out how Lauren's day had gone and had received a very short response, her sister-in-law had said, "I asked Rob what your history was with Cody and he said I should ask you. What happened between the two of you?" Knowing Kim, like Rob, was simply concerned, Lauren had explained briefly. Afterward Kim had responded sympathetically, "That's the kind of thing a girl never forgets, isn't it?"

Cody's apology had touched Lauren, and she knew he was sincere. She imagined it had been difficult for him to say what he'd said.

It was time to forget about what had happened so long ago.

Knowing the kind of day Cody was probably having with Sara underfoot, she asked, "Do you have patient appointments this afternoon?"

"My first patient arrives in ten minutes."

She hesitated only a moment. "Would you like me to come by and pick up Sara? I was going to run out for sandwiches, anyway. I'll have to bring her here with me. Rob's in Denver today, and Mom and Dad are taking care of shipments coming in. But I could play games with her and teach her the names of flowers while I man the office."

"I didn't call for that reason, Lauren." Cody's voice was deep and husky.

"I know." She could sense his hesitation, his determination not to take advantage of her. "I suppose Sara *could* have fun this afternoon seeing each patient with you, asking lots of questions...."

He groaned. "You don't paint a pretty picture."

"Daddy, I'm thirsty. Can I have a drink?" Sara asked from his elbow.

"Nancy keeps orange juice in the refrigerator. As soon as I get off the phone, we'll go get it." After another moment of consideration he asked, "Are you sure you don't mind?"

She really didn't. Actually she looked forward to taking care of Sara. "I don't mind. I'll be over in a few minutes."

After Cody said goodbye and Lauren hung up, she smiled. She shouldn't care about seeing Cody again. She shouldn't be looking forward to the afternoon with Sara. His apology shouldn't have meant so much. But it did. For once in her life she was just going to forget about shoulds and go with the flow. Who knew where that might lead her?

Ten minutes later Lauren was standing in the reception area of Cody and Eli's office, smiling at Nancy. She knew the receptionist because she and Rob and her parents had been under Eli Hasting's care for years. Already two patients were waiting.

"Cody said to send you back to the lounge," Nancy said. "He's getting Sara some juice."

Lauren thanked her, opened the door leading into the examination rooms, then followed the hall to the room in the corner.

When Sara saw Lauren, her face lit up. "Lauren!"

She smiled. "Hi, Sara. Do you want to go to the garden center with me?"

Sara looked up at her dad. "Can I?"

He ruffled her hair fondly. "You sure can. I think you'll have a lot more fun there."

"Can I take my coloring book and crayons?"

When Cody nodded, Sara ran back to Cody's office to get them.

Alone with Cody, Lauren felt a bit awkward after their conversation. Their gazes met and held, and Cody stepped closer. "I should have apologized in person instead of over the phone."

"That's all right," she murmured.

"I hope so," he said seriously, "because I want us to be friends. Sara likes you a lot. And although Kim's good with her, I think having a woman's undivided attention now and then would be good for her, too."

It sounded as if he wanted to be friends for Sara's sake. Why not? She was becoming fond of the little girl. But as she stood close to Cody, breathing in the scent of his aftershave, wanting to brush back a lock of wayward hair over his brow, she realized taking his daughter under her wing could get complicated.

"I haven't forgotten about giving you that motorcycle ride, either. Are you still game?" he asked.

The wind in her hair, her arms around Cody, could possibly give her the thrill of a lifetime. "I'm game," she decided.

She'd never taken risks. For most of her years she'd been sedate rather than impulsive. Maybe it was time she let her hair down, so to speak, and maybe in time her life would become a little more adventurous instead of staid.

Cody's blue gaze seemed almost spellbinding as he reached his hand out toward her cheek. "You're a special woman, Lauren MacMillan."

Before his fingers touched her skin, Sara came running back into the room with her coloring book and crayons. "I'm ready," she proclaimed, almost hopping up and down with the excitement and energy only a four-year-old could exude.

Cody's hand dropped to his side, and Lauren broke eye contact.

For now she would concentrate on Sara. And maybe later...

Maybe later she'd reconsider the risks of being friends with a former football hero who had once stolen her heart.

Chapter Three

Instead of heading home to her apartment on Friday evening, Lauren decided to go to the garden center. Along with Kim and Lindsey, Matt had gotten sick, too, so Lauren had taken care of Sara at Cody's house again today. When he'd gotten home, he'd insisted on taking her to dinner to thank her, with Sara along, of course, since Lauren wouldn't accept any payment for her baby-sitting. There was no way she could accept payment. She loved taking care of Sara.

Dinner had been pleasant, as well as disturbing, whenever her gaze had met Cody's or their fingers had inadvertently touched. They'd kept the conversation casual, but the vibrations between them were anything *but* casual. Part of the time, they'd discussed a backyard pond that he thought Sara would enjoy, and he'd asked Lauren to draw up plans for it. That's why she was headed for her office. She could pick up her catalogs and work on the pond landscaping at home.

When she parked outside the chain-link fence surrounding the nursery area, she saw Rob's pickup truck. The gate was open and she went inside, taking the path to the office. Lights blazed and she opened the door, stepping inside.

Rob was sitting at his desk with the computer on. "I thought you'd be at home. How's Matt?"

"He's feeling better. Dad wanted me to get these receipts into the computer, **and I** didn't have time earlier. Valentine's Day has us scurrying. What are you doing here?"

Valentine's Day was on Sunday and customers would be lined up tomorrow to buy a variety of potted plants decorated with hearts and cupids. Valentine's Day. It was a holiday that was good for winter business. Suddenly she wished it could be a lot more. She wished she could experience the romance associated with it.

As she went to the bookshelves behind her desk, she answered his question. "I just came in for catalogs."

She could feel Rob's gaze on her as he remarked, "Kim told me you took care of Sara again today at Granger's house."

There was a concerned note in her brother's voice. He'd always been protective, and as she looked into his dark-brown eyes now, she knew he would always be that. "Yes, I did. Then Cody asked me to go out to dinner with him and Sara as a thank-you."

"That's all it was?" Rob asked.

"That's all," she answered.

Rob leaned back in his swivel chair and ran his hand through his brown hair. "It sounds as if you might like there to be more."

Her brother could always read her too well. "Maybe I would."

His brows furrowed. "Granger hurt you once before."

"We were teenagers."

"Maybe so. And maybe he was too young to realize what he did to you."

"I did it to myself. I knew he was out of my league. I knew how he felt about Gretchen."

Her brother pushed his chair away from his desk. "Until a few days ago, you didn't seem to want anything to do with the man."

"He apologized for what happened in high school."

"A little late, I'd say," Rob grumbled.

"Rob..."

"Look, Sis, I'm not going to tell you how to live your life. But keep in mind, his wife's only been dead two years."

"Two years is a long time."

"Maybe. Maybe not. Just be careful. I know you liked the guy back then, but he trampled your heart."

"I was young."

"Exactly. It was probably the first time you'd ever really fallen for anybody. And you haven't let yourself fall hard for anyone since, have you?"

She'd gone on dates now and then. She'd even dated an architect, Craig Davis, for a few months. But the truth was—she'd never let herself feel deeply enough about anyone to fall in love. Because of what had happened with Cody? She couldn't be sure of that.

"Don't worry about me, Rob. I'm a big girl now."

"Famous last words," he muttered, and then turned back to his computer.

The sun disappeared behind the spruces as Lauren glanced out the window of her second-floor apartment on Sunday evening. The snow had all melted. She'd worked at the garden center all day with the rush of last-minute Valentine's Day shoppers. But she'd found herself restless, rather than tired, after she returned to her apartment. Working at her drafting table, she had almost completed the finishing touches on the office complex landscaping design when her doorbell rang. She answered it absently, still thinking about her work.

To her amazement Cody stood there, a not-quite smile on his lips. He was wearing jeans and his leather jacket. The width of his shoulders and the wind-blown look of his black hair made her insides quiver.

He spoke before she could find her voice. "I owe you a motorcycle ride."

She'd figured he'd forgotten all about it. She'd figured... "Now?" she asked, the idea thrilling her and scaring her at the same time.

"It's a great night for it." Amusement sparkled in his eyes, and she knew he was daring her.

"Where's Sara?"

"With a teenage neighbor. She baby-sits for me when Kim is busy in the evening."

Suddenly Lauren realized she was being rude by not inviting him inside. "Would you like to come in?"

"Would you like to come out?" he countered with a crooked smile.

She couldn't be a coward. For some reason it seemed necessary that she show Cody she was up to any adventure he might want to tackle. "All right. Just let me get my keys. Do I need anything else?"

His gaze ran over her, from her bangs, down her red sweater, jeans and sneakers. Every second of his perusal increased the trembling inside of her and the vibrations that had been humming just below the surface all last week. "Wear something warm," he suggested.

She doubted that, seated behind Cody with her arms around him, she'd be anything *but* warm. Since she couldn't tell him that, she took her parka from the closet, hung it over her arm, then joined him in the hall, locking the door behind her.

When they finally stood on the curb in front of his motorcycle, Lauren eyed it as if it were a vehicle from another planet.

Cody laughed. "I promise this is going to be fun, Lauren. Trust me."

As she looked up into his eyes, his words took on a deeper meaning than the way he'd meant them. In a sense she'd felt he'd breached her trust so many years ago. They were adults now. Yet she'd never entrusted herself to a man since then. She hadn't entrusted herself to anyone. Independence and self-sufficiency were great defenses against feeling vulnerable.

"I guess I have to wear the helmet," she said, sidestepping his remark.

"Yes, you do." Lifting one of the shiny, blue helmets from the handlebars, he carefully set it on her head, then adjusted the chin strap. His fingers brushed her cheek, and she drew in a breath. His skin was warm, a bit calloused and felt so sensual on hers.

Cody was looking down into her eyes. "How does that feel?" he asked, his voice husky.

"Fine," she managed.

"Then get ready to see the sights of Birch Creek from the back of a bike." Throwing his leg over the seat, he balanced the machine and waited for her to hop on.

Lauren drew her leg over the back of the bike and didn't know what was more unsettling—the powerful bike under her...or the broad expanse of Cody's back before her.

"Once I get it started, put your arms around my waist and hold on. If you want to stop for any reason, just tap me on the shoulder. Got it?"

"Got it," she murmured.

Cody started the bike, and then they were off. In a panic at first, she wondered what had ever possessed her to accept his dare. But then other sensations started taking over. There was the feel of her arms around Cody's body, the sense of motion that soon seemed almost like flying. Then the wind wrapped around her, and the blur of sights seemed different and special as they flew by. Her heart was in her throat, and yet she realized that speeding through Birch Creek on the bike behind Cody made her feel free. It was a freedom of being one with the elements that she'd never experienced before.

The paved roads were smooth for a long time under the bike's wheels as Lauren got caught up in the hum of the excitement and the speed. But then Cody slowed and turned onto a side road that took them past tall pines and fields still frosted here and there with snow. Suddenly a house appeared, and he veered into the parking lot beside it and braked. When his feet went to the ground and he balanced the bike, Lauren climbed off.

Switching off the ignition, he braced the bike. After removing his helmet, he said, "I thought I'd give you time to catch your breath before we started back. How did you like it?"

She unsnapped her helmet and pulled it off. "It was wonderful!"

"I didn't hear any screams, and you didn't tap me on the shoulder, so I hoped you were enjoying it," he said with a grin.

The wind whistled through the spruce and aspen as millions of stars blinked down from the black sky. "I've never felt anything like that. I don't know if it was the speed or the wind. But it was such a rush."

"I know. Whenever I ride, it clears my mind somehow and makes everything more manageable after I get back. Other than that, I just enjoy it."

They were standing in a small gravel parking lot beside an old stone house. There were cars in the lot, and she could see a sign hanging by the walkway to the front door—The Lantern—Dining and Refreshments.

"I've heard about this place," she said. "A couple from Denver bought it and restored it last summer."

"I thought you might like to warm up. They have great espresso and hot chocolate…a restaurant and parlors with fireplaces and lots of old books just sitting around."

"It sounds lovely. But am I dressed okay?"

"It's casual." Taking her helmet from her, he

hung it on the bike with his, and they walked up the path to the front door.

The inside of the house was warm and inviting. A hostess in a long velvet skirt and white ruffled blouse wished them a happy Valentine's Day.

"Do you have a table for two?" Cody asked.

"I'm sorry, sir. We're full up. But we can bring you whatever you'd like in one of the parlors—sandwiches, drinks."

"Hot chocolate is fine for me," Lauren said.

"Two hot chocolates in the parlor then," Cody told the hostess with a smile.

The woman led them down a short hall into a sitting room where the walls were covered in antique-looking wallpaper splashed with large roses. A fire burned in the fireplace, and the huge rough-hewn mantel was decorated with old bottles of different colors and shapes. A large, heart-shaped wreath made of grapevines hung in the center of it. Two love seats, covered in forest-green crushed velvet, and curved-back occasional chairs sat near marble-topped tables upon which lay leather-bound books.

"This is charming."

"I hoped you'd like it."

Lauren looked up into his blue eyes, and a thrill of anticipation rushed through her. It was Valentine's Day and she was here with Cody. He seemed glad to be with her.

When she unzipped her parka, he helped slide it from her shoulders. His hand brushed her arm, and when she looked at him again, there was the same awareness in his eyes that she felt. Had he offered her this motorcycle ride tonight simply as a thank-you? Or did he want more?

After he hung their coats on an old-fashioned wooden clothes tree, they sat on the love seat facing the fireplace.

"The Lantern has three rooms like this," he said. "So they never get overcrowded, even when guests are waiting to be seated in the dining room. When the weather is nice, you can wander through the gardens outside."

Fire leaped in the brick fireplace, the flames golden and orange and giving off warmth. It created an atmosphere of intimacy that wound around them. Sitting next to Cody like this, Lauren didn't need the fire for warmth.

A waitress carrying a tray with a small plate of cookies and two tall mugs of hot chocolate topped with whipped cream came in and set the tray on the coffee table. "Happy Valentine's Day."

"Thank you," Cody and Lauren said together, and then looked at each other and smiled.

After the waitress left, Cody gazed down at Lauren for a moment and then stood. "Don't move. I'll be right back."

While Cody was gone, Lauren took the time to scan the room again. A gold Cupid sat on a pedestal table near the window, and a garland of tiny red hearts draped across the curtain valance.

Valentine's Day hadn't meant very much to her in the past. She always sent her parents a Valentine...and Kim and Rob...just to let them know she loved them. But the holiday had never meant anything romantic for her. Until today.

When Cody returned to the room, he was carrying a long-stemmed red rose. As he lowered himself onto the love seat next to her once again, he handed it to her. "This is for you."

"Oh, Cody. It's beautiful." She bent her head to the petals. It had a lovely scent. Roses were her favorite flowers.

Wanting to know more about the man Cody was now, she asked, "What else do you do for fun…besides riding your motorcycle?"

"Mostly spend time with Sara, shoot hoops, play chess with Eli. What about you?"

"I spend a lot of time with Rob and Kim, Lindsey and Matt. In the summers we go camping together. And I have friends. One of them, Eve Coleburn, just had a baby in January. I love holding her new daughter. But other than that…mostly I work or curl up with a good book."

She brushed the rose petal against her cheek. It was so wonderfully soft. When she looked up, she saw that Cody was watching her very intently. And in his eyes…

Could that be desire?

"We'd better drink our hot chocolate before the whipped cream melts," he said with a nod toward the table.

They picked up their mugs. Lauren sipped at hers, the whipped cream covering her lips. As she lowered the mug, Cody reached out and brushed his thumb along her upper lip.

When he pulled away, there was whipped cream on his thumb, and he licked it off. The gesture was incredibly sensual, and she tingled all over. What would it be like to kiss Cody again, to be held in his arms, to discover if he was attracted to her now, the same way she'd always been attracted to him?

As they drank the chocolate, they stared into the fire, acutely aware of the silence, the rose on her lap, the heart wreath above the mantel.

They set down their mugs at the same time, and then Lauren turned toward Cody. "Thank you for taking me riding tonight. For bringing me here." She lifted the rose. "And for this."

His eyes became a deeper blue. "No thanks are necessary," he murmured, looking down at her with an intensity she remembered...with an intensity that drew her closer to him.

He slipped his hand under her hair and bent his head. When his lips came down on hers, she felt as if she were caught up in the speed of racing with the wind again. Old memories rushed into new sensations as his mouth became more possessive and then opened over hers.

There was nothing in this universe like Cody's kiss. As his tongue masterfully stroked hers, she lifted her arms around his neck, and her breasts grazed his chest. His hard body pressing against hers was as erotic as the fusing of their mouths. Cody's hands caressed her back, and she slid her fingers into the hair at his nape. The texture of it was thick and soft. She inhaled his scent, lost in the moment and the pleasure. His low groan told her of his arousal as much as the tension in his body.

But then he abruptly broke the kiss and leaned away, breathing as raggedly as she was.

"Cody?" she asked, not sure if she had imagined the desire or if it had been truly there.

"We'd better finish our chocolate and start back," he said, his voice gravelly.

She knew he was probably thinking about getting

home to Sara, but she wished to heaven she knew what else he was thinking. Had the kiss meant anything to him? Was he going to pretend it hadn't happened? Was he thinking of Gretchen and the passion he'd shared with her? Had Lauren simply been convenient, as she had been once before?

But she couldn't put the questions into words. She couldn't be humiliated again by having him tell her this kiss had meant nothing.

Lifting her chin, she agreed, "Yes, we should be getting back."

A few minutes later they'd set their empty mugs on the table and left the cookies untouched. When they stood, there was an awkwardness between them that hadn't been there before. She didn't regret kissing him. Yet she knew better than to weave dreams where Cody Granger was concerned.

As he helped her with her coat, she glanced at him over her shoulder. The warmth was gone from his expression. His eyes were an inscrutable blue that gave no sign as to what he was thinking or feeling. Zippering her parka, she knew the ride back to her apartment wouldn't be as sweet as the ride here had been.

She also knew that giving her heart to Cody Granger again could be more dangerous than riding his bike at 100 miles an hour with no brakes.

A few days later Lauren parked in Cody's driveway, the ideas for his pond and garden on the seat beside her. She'd tried to put his kiss out of her mind, but couldn't. When he'd taken her back to her apartment Sunday night, she hadn't invited him in. After he'd left, it had taken a long while to shake off the aftereffects of being held in his arms...of feeling his lips on hers once again.

And now...

They had to clear the air. Using the excuse of dropping off the sketches for his backyard had seemed like a good idea while she was working at the garden center. Now she wasn't so sure.

Climbing out of the van, she went to his front door and rang the bell.

Sara came running toward the screen. "Daddy's on the phone," she announced.

Lauren was debating whether or not to step inside when Cody, dressed in a suit and tie, came into the foyer and opened the door.

"I probably should have called," Lauren began, "but I thought I'd drop off the sketches I made for your backyard."

He raked his hand through his hair. "The pond."

She nodded, then asked, "Is this a bad time?"

"I just got off the phone with my baby-sitter. Kim had a hairdresser's appointment, so I lined up Debbie. I've always found her dependable, but not tonight. Her boyfriend surprised her with tickets for a concert. I'm supposed to leave in five minutes to attend a meeting in Denver about an HMO."

"Is the meeting important?"

"Eli thinks it is. He's tied up tonight and asked me to sit in."

Sara tugged on Cody's arm. "Lauren can stay, can't you, Lauren? I like her better. Debbie watches TV."

Cody crouched down beside his daughter. "I'm going to skip the meeting tonight. I'm sure Lauren has other plans."

She wanted to talk to him, but she knew now wasn't the time for a personal conversation. If she stayed with Sara, they could talk when he got back. "Actually, I don't have plans. I'd be glad to stay."

Standing, he shook his head. "I won't impose on you again."

"I told you before, spending time with Sara isn't an imposition."

Finally Cody glanced at his watch, then agreed. "All right. But when I get home, we're going to have to figure out a barter system. Your time is valuable, too."

Lauren knew her time was valuable, but she also realized that the reason she didn't want Cody to repay her was that she liked spending time with him and his daughter...maybe liked it entirely too much.

It was almost 2:00 a.m. when Cody pulled into his garage. He'd never expected to get home this late. He'd been driving back from the meeting that had dragged on forever when he'd been paged. Two of his patients were in the emergency room—one with abdominal distress, the other with chest pains. He'd called Lauren, and she'd told him not to worry about it. She would snooze on his couch if he was late.

He was late, all right. The abdominal distress had been appendicitis, the chest pains had been a minor heart attack, and he'd gotten tied up for hours.

Now he was returning home to Lauren, still vividly remembering her arms around him on the bike ride, as well as the kiss that had practically knocked him out of his boots. It had disconcerted him so much he'd needed time to think about it. But thinking about it had brought sleepless nights...and un-satisfied arousal.

Frustrated with the desire for Lauren that had broadsided him for the past week, he closed the door to his SUV and went into the kitchen. The light shone over the sink, but he didn't hear the murmur of the TV. When he reached the living room, he stopped still. Lauren was sleeping on the couch on her side, her hair splayed across a large throw pillow. Nestled in, she looked comfortable. When he gently called her name, she didn't awaken.

If he woke her up now, he would disturb her deep sleep. Deciding it would be kinder to let her sleep through the night on his couch, he went back to the kitchen, wrote a note that he was home and took it to the coffee table where Lauren would see it if she awakened before morning.

But he couldn't make himself move away from her. He couldn't seem to stop staring at her—the delicate tilt of her nose, her refined chin, the curve of her cheekbones. And then there was her mouth. He remembered how she'd responded so passionately...so sweetly.

Taking a throw from the back of the recliner, he gently spread it over her, tempted to lean down and kiss her cheek...so tempted to do more.

But it was late, and he was tired, and he had no intention of satisfying his own lust at Lauren's expense. After a last, long look at her, he switched off the small table light and headed for the stairs.

If Cody thought he'd fall asleep quickly, he was wrong. He tossed and turned until dawn, tangling the covers, much too aware of Lauren downstairs in his living room. Finally he fell into a fitful sleep.

The door chimes awakened him.

Out of habit he checked the clock. It was 7:30 a.m., and he'd forgotten to set his alarm. Who could be at the door at this time of the morning? Dressed only in sleeping shorts he went down the steps and hurried to the door.

When he opened it, Dolores DeWitt said, "My goodness! You're not even dressed yet."

"I had a late night." Why in the hell was she at his door at this time of the morning? "Is something wrong?"

Opening the door before *he* could, she pushed inside. "Not exactly. I just wanted to spend some time with my granddaughter since you don't seem inclined to bring her to visit." Her tone was accusatory.

He'd checked his schedule with Eli and found he could get away for a day this weekend. But he hadn't gotten a chance to call Dolores yet. As always she looked elegant this morning. She was in her late fifties. Her platinum hair was styled in a pageboy, and her pale-blue wool coat and matching slacks probably sported designer labels. A trust fund from her father as well as a generous divorce settlement subsidized her expensive tastes.

But this surprise visit of hers was unusual, and he wondered what it was about. "You showed up this early because you want to spend the day with Sara?"

"Actually, I want to take her on a little jaunt. There's a children's theater in—" Suddenly Dolores stopped when she looked into the living room and saw Lauren, who was now standing by the couch, looking sleep tousled and delectable.

"Who is *she?*" Dolores demanded to know. "And

what's she doing in your house at this hour of the morning?''

Dolores's attitude angered Cody. ''That's none of your business, Dolores.''

''It is *entirely* my business. My granddaughter's welfare is my business. You spend long hours away from her. You don't give her the advantages she should have, and you make her sleep in that room upstairs that's barely furnished.'' Dolores swept her hand around his first floor. ''You don't even have dishes in your china cupboard, for goodness' sakes. Sara needs someone who can give her everything she deserves, as well as full-time attention. I've been thinking about suing for custody for a long time now, and this morning I see I even have more grounds. Your bachelor lifestyle isn't one a child should be around.''

Cody had rarely known true fear. There was no place for it in decisions he made about his patients or in the way he lived his life. But now it gripped him so hard his chest tightened. Dolores had money, lots of it. Gaining custody of Sara could be a cause she would pursue with a vengeance. He knew he was a good father, but he also knew he couldn't make up for Sara not having a mother.

And he did work long hours. Dolores might have the grounds to take his daughter away.

He *wouldn't* let that happen. He had to stop her in her tracks right now and then consult a lawyer and do whatever he had to do to keep Sara with him.

With a glance at Lauren, who was running her fingers through her hair, he said to Dolores, ''Lauren isn't just any woman. She's my fiancée.''

Chapter Four

"**Y**our fiancée? Since when?" Dolores demanded to know.

Cody knew he had no right to expect Lauren to go along with this. But he prayed she would for the sake of his daughter. "Lauren's sister-in-law has been taking care of Sara since I returned to Birch Creek. And Lauren and I went to school together. When we ran into each other at Kim's, we renewed our friendship and found there was a lot more."

His gaze sought Lauren's. Everything he'd said was true, including the discovery of the chemistry between them.

Dolores's lips pursed as she looked from Cody to Lauren. "And just when is the wedding?"

Before Cody could respond, Lauren came toward them. It was up to her now, to either go on with the charade or let it blow up in his face.

Her elbow brushed his as she stood very close, the way an engaged couple might stand. "We haven't set a date yet, Mrs. DeWitt.'' Then Lauren extended her hand to his mother-in-law. "I'm Lauren Mac-Millan.''

But instead of shaking Lauren's hand, Dolores shook her finger at Cody. "If you think you're going to wipe Gretchen's memory from Sara's mind, you're sadly mistaken. And if you think you can keep me away from my granddaughter, you're wrong about that, too. I intend to discuss this situation with my lawyer and proceed from there."

"There's no reason to bring lawyers into this. We both want what's best for Sara." Cody knew staying calm was the best way to deal with Dolores. But it was damn hard to do.

"*I* want what's best for Sara. You don't *know* what's best for Sara." She turned toward the still-opened door. "I have rights, Cody, and I'm not going to let you cut me out of my granddaughter's life. I'll be in touch." With that she flounced out the door.

After Dolores started her car and backed out of Cody's driveway, he raked his hand through his hair and looked at Lauren. "I never should have put you in that position, but I had to try to stop her from going ahead with the custody issue."

Lauren searched his face, then admitted, "That's why I backed you up. But what are you going to do when she finds out we're not engaged?"

"I don't know. But at least this will buy me some time. I'll make an appointment to see Barry Sentz and get legal advice on what I should do." He and Barry had renewed their friendship from high school when Cody returned to Birch Creek. They played basketball together as often as they could, but

Barry's law practice kept him as busy as Cody's medical practice did.

Lauren was still standing very close to Cody. Her hair was sleep tousled, her deep-brown eyes filled with concern. "Anyone who looks can see that Sara belongs with you."

After a glance upstairs to where his daughter slept, he shook his head. "It's not that simple anymore. Sometimes the person with the most money or influence wins these lawsuits. I'd hock everything I own to fight for Sara, but I don't know if that will be enough. Dolores *can* give the undivided attention to Sara that I can't."

"You do give her your undivided attention when you're with her."

"Ah, but that's the thing. I have a medical practice. Dolores doesn't have to work."

Lightly touching his arm, Lauren assured him, "It'll be all right, Cody. I know it will."

Her touch on his skin was meant to be comforting, but it stirred up the fire that smoldered between them. "I never intended to drag you into this. I'll see Barry and get this settled. Thanks again for backing me up this morning."

"I did it for Sara," Lauren said softly.

Their gazes met for a few moments...and held.

Then Lauren backed away from him. "I'd better be going. I need to stop at my apartment and shower and change before I go to the garden center."

She slipped on her parka, then picked up her purse as well as her briefcase from where it stood near the sofa. "Let me know what Barry Sentz says."

"I will."

As Cody said goodbye to Lauren and watched her

leave his house, he thought again about Dolores's threat and what he was going to do about it. He'd do anything to keep his daughter with him.

Anything.

Throughout the day Lauren thought about what had happened at Cody's house that morning, and heard the echo of his voice as he told his mother-in-law she was his fiancée. It had been almost like glimpsing a dream through a curtain. But she knew if she stepped through the curtain, the dream would vanish. He'd been trying to protect his daughter, and Lauren had understood that right away. That's why she'd gone along with him.

As the afternoon wore on, Lauren glanced at the office clock often, wondering if Cody had seen Barry Sentz yet. When she thought of Barry, she was reminded again of that day when she'd caught Cody kissing Gretchen. Barry had been one of the onlookers. He'd been the one who'd noticed Lauren watching Cody kiss his high school sweetheart. Lauren hadn't crossed paths with Barry since, because they moved in different circles.

Why couldn't she let go of what had happened after all these years?

Because you loved Cody Granger, and he didn't love you.

She scolded herself for even thinking it. She'd had a crush on Cody. She hadn't loved him. She hadn't even known what love was. Maybe she still didn't.

The heating unit in Lauren's office hummed as she went over the plans for her most-recent landscaping job. When there was a rap on her door, she called, "Come in."

Expecting Rob or her mom or dad, her heart beat faster when Cody entered. He was wearing a charcoal suit with a gray-and-white tie, but the collar of his shirt was unbuttoned and the tie tugged down. "I saw Barry," he said without preamble.

"What did he say?"

Cody lowered himself into the chair beside her desk. Even seated, he was tall and broad-shouldered and made the office seem very small. "He said that grandparents are winning custody suits, and that in this case, being a doctor could work against me because of the hours and the frequency of being called away unexpectedly. It's a crapshoot, depending on the judge. He also told me that a custody suit in itself, even if I win, will cause a terrific upheaval in my life and Sara's."

"Oh, Cody." Lauren's heart went out to him. She knew how much he loved his daughter. "What are you going to do?"

Cody's expression became unreadable as his gaze settled on hers and locked. "According to Barry, the best thing I can do is to get married and create a stable home so Dolores has no grounds for a suit. I drove around for a while before I came here, thinking about it. I know Barry's right." After a pause he went on, "I'll do anything I have to do to keep Sara with me."

Lauren's heart raced at the intensity in his eyes and what his decision meant. "You're going to get married?"

"That depends. I'd only marry someone I know would be good for Sara...good *with* Sara. And I can only think of one person who fits the bill." He paused. "You. Will you marry me, Lauren?"

It seemed as if a thousand thoughts clicked through Lauren's mind at one time. Her idea of a proposal, when and if it ever happened to her, included music and flowers and head-over-heels love that only happened once in a lifetime. But then she thought about taking care of Sara last week—reading to her, playing with her, tucking her in for her nap. Last of all, she remembered kissing Cody...her inexperience with men...intimacies in a marriage bed.

With the vision in her head, heat flooded her cheeks. "You can't be serious!"

Squarely meeting her gaze, Cody assured her, "I've never been more serious. I can provide a good home for us, Lauren. I can promise fidelity and loyalty and commitment."

But what about love? a voice inside of her screamed. She had feelings for Cody, but they were all mixed up—past and present. And what kind of feelings did he have for her? Could they build a friendship into something more? "Marriage can't be your only option."

"It's my only option if I want to keep Sara and prevent the trauma of a custody suit." He reached across the desk and took Lauren's hand. "I know we can make it work."

His hand on hers made her feel safe, made her feel as if his proposal wasn't the most outlandish idea in all the world. "But what if we just pretended to be engaged?" she asked.

"Dolores is an intelligent woman, and we couldn't pretend forever. I'm going to see if she and I can come to an understanding. But if I get the sense that she's still going to see a lawyer and take this to court,

I'll have to do something. I love Sara more than my life, and I won't let her be taken away from me.''

The way Gretchen had been taken away from him? He had already lost his wife, and she could see that he couldn't bear to lose his daughter. But marriage? A marriage of convenience?

Releasing her hand, he stood. ''Think about it, Lauren. Give it a lot of thought. I'll be in touch.''

And before she could gather her thoughts enough to come up with an adequate reply, he was gone.

Should she even consider his crazy proposal?

She already was.

Lauren was eating breakfast the next morning when her phone rang. Coffee mug in hand, she picked it up.

''Lauren, it's Cody.''

She hadn't slept much last night thinking about his proposal...Sara...what a marriage could mean. ''I haven't decided yet,'' she said softly.

''Dolores called.''

His voice was even and controlled, but she sensed the turmoil underlying it. ''What did she want?''

''To inform me that if you're really my fiancée, she wants to get to know you better. She suggested we come to dinner on Sunday.''

''It's a test, isn't it?'' Lauren asked.

''Yes.''

''What did you tell her?''

''That I'd check with you and see what your plans were. Are you free?''

''If we go...if we pretend we're engaged...do you think it will do any good?''

''I think if she sees we're a couple, and that we're

planning a life together, she might back down. At least it will give me a chance to talk with her and assure her I'll let her spend time with Sara. If I do that, maybe she'll forget about a custody suit. In the meantime why don't we spend some time together this week? In fact, there's a puppet show in the mall tonight. Would you like to go with Sara and me?"

In not so many words, he was suggesting that they practice for Sunday. Whether she decided to accept his proposal or not, she could help him out with this...for Sara's sake. "The puppet show sounds like fun. Do you want me to meet you there?"

"No, we'll pick you up. Around seven?"

"Seven sounds good."

When Lauren put down the receiver, she realized she was excited about tonight. Cody Granger's marriage proposal didn't seem quite as far-fetched as it had last night.

On Sunday the February day was full of sun, blue sky and the clear cold of winter. But as Cody drove to Colorado Springs, Lauren could feel the tension in him and in herself. Neither of them had spoken of his proposal again while they'd gone to the puppet show with Sara and made her the center of their attention. She'd watched with such gleeful enthusiasm that she'd captured Lauren's heart completely.

The following evening Cody had invited Lauren for a late supper. Afterward Sara had pleaded with Lauren to stay and put her to bed. Unable to resist, Lauren had agreed, and as she'd read a story to Sara, Cody had sat in a nearby chair watching and ever mindful. He hadn't kissed her or touched her since

Valentine's Day, but that only added to the highly charged atmosphere between them.

She couldn't help thinking about what it would be like to be his wife and to share his bed. An intense look in his eyes told her he was thinking about the same thing.

Last evening he'd been on call, but they'd taken Sara to a children's movie. It was obvious that if they married, Sara would be the reason why.

Now as Cody turned into a development with large brick pillars at its entrance, Lauren studied the houses. Some were huge, some weren't. All of them had an elegance about them that told her this was, indeed, an elite residential area. Dolores DeWitt's home was a sprawling brick rancher, connected by a breezeway to the garage.

After Cody pulled into the driveway and switched off the ignition, he turned to Lauren. "We have to make this convincing."

Lauren nodded, knowing his future with Sara depended on it.

When Dolores opened the door, her expression was grave until her glance fell on Sara. Then she crouched down and said to her, "I think you've grown two inches."

"I'll soon be as big as Daddy," Sara proclaimed proudly.

Straightening, Dolores took Sara's hand. "Clara has dinner almost ready. Why don't we go into the living room? I have a present for Sara."

Cody spoke then. "Dolores, I told you it's not a good idea to give her a present every time you see her."

"It's just something little," she said breezily, as

she eyed Lauren in her camel coat and forest-green wool skirt that almost skimmed her ankles.

"Come in," she told them. "I have hors d'oeuvres and drinks waiting."

As they walked through the ceramic-tiled foyer, Cody draped his arm around Lauren's shoulders. For a moment she tensed, then she realized that they had to playact, they had to pretend to be a loving, engaged couple. Cody's body was warm and strong against hers, and their hips bumped as they walked. He was wearing a navy-and-tan-striped sweater and jeans. As usual, just looking at him made her tremble inside.

In Dolores's pale-mauve living room, they sat on the sofa together, close enough that Lauren wondered if Cody could hear her heart beat.

While Sara busily opened the present that Dolores handed her, Dolores motioned to the silver carafe of coffee on a tray on the chrome-and-glass coffee table, as well as the stuffed mushrooms and tiny quiches. "Help yourself."

Lauren couldn't eat a bite, not with her stomach flipflopping as Cody laid his hand possessively on her knee. "What would you like?"

"Um, nothing right now, thanks."

Sara finished opening her present and made quick work of the lid and the tissue paper, pulling out a soft-looking doll. Running to Cody and Lauren, she said, "See what I got!"

Dolores said, "Push her tummy, and she'll say lots of things to you."

Sara did as Dolores instructed and giggled as the doll talked to her. Fascinated, she took it about ten feet away and sat down on the floor and pressed its stomach again.

"What do you say, Sara?" Cody prompted.

"Thank you, Grammy."

"You're most welcome, darling." As Sara examined the doll more carefully, Dolores's attention focused on Lauren. "So...tell me about yourself. What keeps you busy in Birch Creek?"

"I'm a landscape architect. I work at my parents' garden center."

"Isn't that convenient. You had a ready-made position waiting for you when you finished school and didn't have to strike out on your own."

It was a veiled insult and apparently Cody wasn't standing for it. "MacMillan's Garden Center is a family business, Dolores. Lauren's brother works there, too. The MacMillans are very tight-knit. Something rare in this day and age."

"Maybe so." Dolores brushed a nonexistent piece of lint from her slacks as she regrouped. "Just how long have you and Cody been dating?"

It wasn't Lauren's nature to lie, so she carefully chose the truth. "We didn't start out officially dating. I took care of Sara when my sister-in-law was sick and things just sort of developed from there."

Dolores's housekeeper came to the living room, announcing that dinner was ready. Thankful the inquisition had ended for the time being, Lauren was unprepared for Cody's hand engulfing hers as he stood and waited for her to rise, too. *We're putting on a show for Dolores DeWitt,* she reminded herself. Yet the heat of his hand covering hers sent tingles dancing throughout her body.

Over dinner Dolores described to Cody the new

wing being added to a hospital in Colorado Springs. "It will be the best emergency care center around, with every technological advantage. Gretchen did such a wonderful job raising money for it."

To Lauren Dolores explained, "Gretchen and Cody were the perfect couple. My daughter worked side by side with Cody to help the quality of health care in this community. Everyone loved her so, and she could convince anyone to believe in the same causes she did. Couldn't she, Cody?"

After a pause he said, "Yes, she could."

"This community respected my daughter and everything she did for it."

Lauren didn't know what to say to that. Apparently Gretchen had been not only beautiful and charming, but community conscious, too. It sounded as if she'd done everything well. Old insecurities nudged Lauren, and she wondered how she could ever compete with that.

After dinner Dolores went into the kitchen to speak to her housekeeper, and Sara followed along. Cody took Lauren into the sitting room with a fireplace. A floor-to-ceiling palladium window overlooking the backyard created a dramatic effect. They wandered toward it, appreciating the manicured gardens.

"How are you holding up?" he asked, concerned.

She glanced up at him. "I'm fine."

There was a noise at the archway between the kitchen and the sitting room. Cody leaned close to Lauren and whispered in her ear, "I think we're being watched. We'd better do something about that."

And before she could ask what, his arms went around her and his lips came down forcefully on hers. She reminded herself this wasn't a real kiss, it was a pretend kiss. It was a theatrical kiss because someone was watching them. But the firmness of Cody's lips as well as the sensual invasion of his tongue took her breath away in spite of everything she was telling herself.

When he ended it, his breathing was as quick and shallow as hers. But his blue eyes revealed no emotion as he said in a low voice, "That should do it."

Lauren realized this trap of pretense was a lot more dangerous for her than it was for him. Backing away from him, she murmured, "I'd better check on Sara."

It wasn't much of an escape, but it was all she could think of right now. Avoiding his gaze, she hurried into the kitchen.

When Lauren entered, Dolores stared at her flushed face. "You didn't tell me exactly how long you and Cody have been dating."

The woman didn't miss a thing. "In some ways it seems like a very short time, and in others as if we've been dating forever. I guess that comes from knowing each other in high school," Lauren said glibly, though she was feeling anything but glib.

Pointedly Dolores looked at the ring finger of Lauren's left hand. "You say you're engaged, but I don't see an engagement ring."

Lauren lifted her chin a little higher. "With Cody's schedule and mine, we just haven't had time to go looking for one yet." The explanation sounded reasonable, even to her, but she didn't want to be grilled by Dolores for very long. "Have you seen Sara? I wouldn't want her to get into anything she shouldn't."

"She's in the living room listening to her new doll. It's a shame Cody doesn't buy her new toys more often."

"Children don't need a lot of toys to be happy, Mrs. DeWitt. Cody gives Sara his attention and his love, and that's what matters."

Dolores's mouth opened as if she hadn't expected such an honest response, and Lauren took advantage of the pause to slip away.

But she didn't find Sara in the living room, so she called the little girl's name.

"I'm here." The tiny voice came from down the hall.

Lauren stepped into a room furnished with an elegant mahogany library-style desk and floor-to-ceiling bookshelves. Sara was seated in the cream leather swivel chair, turning herself around and around. "I like this chair," she explained with a huge grin. "It's like a merry-go-round."

Lauren laughed. "I suppose so. But I don't know if you should be in here." Sara's new doll was lying on the desk on a stack of papers. As Lauren picked it up, the papers slid to the floor.

Coming up beside Lauren, Sara took the doll from her. "I'll go tell Daddy I took a ride on the chair." She ran out of the office and down the hall through the living room with her usual exuberant energy.

Smiling, Lauren stooped to pick up the papers that had fallen. They became reshuffled when she gathered them up, and as she laid them on the desk and straightened them, she glanced at the top one. It was a letter to Dolores from her attorney.

She shouldn't read it, she told herself. But she was already glancing over the words, and one sentence made her stiffen in anger. "If you pursue filing for custody, I'll make sure Judge Porter handles the case since you and he are friends. He would give us the advantage we would need."

Advantage?

Knowing the judge wasn't an advantage; it was unethical.

Is this what Cody had meant by Dolores's influence? Did she know more than one judge? Wouldn't that color the way the magistrate looked at the case? No wonder Cody didn't want to risk having this go to court. No wonder he was so certain he had to do something now before it even got started.

As Lauren went through the kitchen to the parlor, she made her decision about marrying Cody and protecting his relationship with Sara.

Sara was occupied with a stack of puzzles kept on the lower shelf of the square coffee table in front of the love seat. Lauren went to sit beside Cody, preparing herself for anything Dolores might throw their way.

After a few moments of inconsequential conversation, Dolores straightened in her chair. "We might as well get to what we're all thinking about. I saw my lawyer."

"And?" Cody asked in a perfectly calm voice.

"And...if you two are really going to get married, I won't challenge your custody of Sara. My lawyer tells me it would be too difficult to win. On the other hand, if this is some kind of charade for my benefit, I will have grounds to go to court. So I need one piece of important information from you. When is the wedding date?"

Chapter Five

Cody knew the moment of truth had come. He'd asked Lauren to marry him to protect his daughter, but he wouldn't force her into something she didn't want. He'd just have to—

"We're going to set the wedding date tonight," Lauren responded to his mother-in-law's question.

Cody's gaze locked to Lauren's. Was she bluffing...or did she mean it?

"Would you like a calendar?" Dolores asked sweetly, as if she didn't believe Lauren was serious.

"We'd rather do it in private," Cody answered. "I'll let you know what we decide."

"That will be wonderful." Dolores's tone of voice belied her words. "Do you think you'll have your wedding outdoors again?"

He had never known Dolores to be malicious, but her question was inappropriate, and he knew she knew it. His wedding to Gretchen had taken place outside, in a hotel's courtyard. If Dolores was trying to goad him into some kind of outburst she could use against him, he wouldn't let her succeed. He was too concerned about Lauren and her feelings and what was going on in her head.

"Lauren and I will toss around ideas and see what's best for us."

Dolores's expression changed from confrontational to deeply sad. He knew if he remarried, he'd be moving on while she'd be left in the past with her grief. In spite of the problems in his marriage, Gretchen's death had left a hole in his life, too. Compassion for the older woman led him to say, "I know this has to be difficult for you, Dolores."

For a moment she looked surprised that he understood and then just terribly unhappy. "Yes, it is. I expected you and Gretchen to have a long, happy marriage."

He and Gretchen hadn't been happy, though he'd tried hard to make it otherwise. He'd wanted an intimacy Gretchen had never understood. He'd wanted a future with more children, and Gretchen hadn't. Most of the time he'd been aware that she regretted having Sara because Sara had tied her down. Whenever he had come home to find that Gretchen had left their little girl with Dolores or a baby-sitter again...

Just then, Sara came running over to Lauren and Cody. But instead of sitting next to her father, she went to Lauren and leaned her head on her knee.

Lauren gently stroked Sara's hair. "Tired, little one?" she asked.

Nodding, Sara kept her head in Lauren's lap.

The tableau touched Cody, and he knew what a wonderful mother Lauren would make—if she agreed to marry him—if she'd meant what she said about setting a wedding date.

"We'd better go," he said, his voice husky. "Sara will probably nap in the car on the way home."

Standing, Dolores said stiffly, "It was a pleasure meeting you, Lauren. If you marry Cody, I'm sure we'll be seeing more of each other." To Cody she said, "Please call me as soon as you set the date."

"We'll do that." He had the feeling Dolores would be consulting with her lawyer again to line up her next maneuver if the wedding didn't take place soon.

Fifteen minutes later Sara was asleep in the back seat, cuddling her new doll, as Cody drove home to Birch Creek. Glancing in the rearview mirror, he remembered his daughter resting her head on Lauren's knee and Lauren's tender stroking of her hair. Lauren had been extremely quiet since they'd left Dolores DeWitt's house.

"You can still back out of this," he said.

"Have you changed your mind about your proposal?"

He took a few moments to determine again if his decision was a good one. "No. But I know what marriage is, Lauren. It's a serious step. I want you to be sure it's a step you want to take."

After a short silence Lauren responded, "I made up my mind about marrying you when I saw something in Dolores's office."

"What?"

"It was a letter from her lawyer. I wasn't snooping, but I'd knocked a few papers to the floor, and when I picked them up, I saw it." She told him what the letter said.

He swore. "I know Dolores has influence. That's what worried me about this from the start."

"If we get married, you won't have to worry about it anymore."

He glanced over at her. "Are you sure it's what you want?"

She answered his question with one of her own. "Do you really think a marriage between us can work?"

All afternoon he'd wanted to pull Lauren into his arms and kiss her again. All afternoon, he'd thought about having her in his bed at night. Glad they weren't on the interstate yet, he pulled over to the side of the road and put the SUV in park. Then he unhooked his seat belt and very deliberately unfastened hers. Curving his arm around her shoulders, he nudged her to him. As he gazed down at her upturned lips, he was filled with desire and ready to let their passion take fire. Without hesitating, he covered her lips with his...coaxing...seducing...exploring. He kissed first one corner of her mouth and then the other, until she moaned softly and opened to him. His tongue swept over hers and then forayed. With a fervent response she laced her hand into his hair until he was entirely too mindful of where they were and the fact that Sara was sleeping in the back seat.

Reluctantly he broke the kiss. "There's fire between us, Lauren. And yes, I think this marriage can work. We have a common goal—Sara's happiness. I can offer you a comfortable life, good standing in the community and a daughter to love. Will you be my wife?"

Her eyes were hazy with the passion they'd shared, but there was no uncertainty in her voice when she answered. "Yes, I'll be your wife."

Something in him came alive at her words, but he told himself he was just relieved. "I think we should get married as soon as possible. We can go to a justice of the peace."

After a pause Lauren answered, "That's fine."

Glad they'd settled everything but the date, Cody refastened his seat belt, and Lauren did the same with hers. Then he started the car and headed for home.

Lauren thought about being married in front of a justice of the peace as they drove back to Birch Creek. As a little girl, she'd dreamed of a wedding with attendants and tuxedos, and a gown fit for a princess. She was an adult now and had to face reality. She couldn't have romantic illusions about a marriage born of convenience. She did have hopes, though. Her feelings for Cody were growing stronger each day, and she hoped his would grow stronger for her, too.

From Cody's devotion to his daughter, Lauren knew he was the type of man who could keep promises and who understood their value. She had no doubt that he'd do everything in his power to make this marriage work. So would she. She might not be able to compete with Gretchen in style or flair or beauty, but she could bring warmth into Cody's house and make it a real home for him and Sara.

While trying to imagine her life with Cody, Lauren hardly registered driving through Birch Creek until he pulled into his driveway.

"Sara's still sleeping," he said. "I'm going to try

to carry her in without waking her, and let her finish her nap.''

The four-year-old didn't wake up as Cody carried her through the garage into the kitchen and up the stairs. Lauren was waiting for him in the living room when he came back down a few minutes later.

He lowered himself beside her on the sofa. ''When I mentioned the justice of the peace earlier, I was thinking about convenience and not much else. But this is your wedding, too, Lauren. Is a civil ceremony what you want?''

From experiencing her parents' marriage, as well as Rob and Kim's, Lauren knew the most important element was honesty. That honesty had to start here and now. ''I understand if you don't want an elaborate ceremony, but I really would like to get married before a minister in a church. And I know my parents would like that, too.''

''In a church,'' he repeated, looking down at her with guarded eyes. ''I don't know if we can find one on short notice, but we can try.''

''I can call my minister,'' she offered. ''Maybe he can fit in an evening service. We can keep the guest list limited...just have something small.''

''I belong to Briarwood Club. They have rooms for wedding receptions.''

''I hear Briarwood's lovely.'' Briarwood had a golf course and health club facilities, and she knew many of the professionals in Birch Creek belonged to it. ''Are you sure that's what you want, too?''

''It doesn't matter to me, Lauren. I think weddings and all the trappings are more important to women than to men.''

Lauren was getting the feeling that Cody just

wanted to get this over with. Was that any way to start their married life? Yet their reason for marrying was different from that of most couples.

Cody continued, ''When Sara wakes up from her nap, let's go tell your parents, and Kim and Rob. Then we can find out if your church is free. I'll bet if we put our minds to it, we can have all of the arrangements finished by the end of the week.''

He was being so practical, so...removed. But maybe when they actually got into the planning that would change. And maybe when they kissed again—

If and when they *did* kiss again, she'd figure out whether she was protecting Sara or whether she was following her own heart.

After Lauren's family recovered from the shock of Lauren and Cody's announcement that they were getting married as soon as they could arrange it, her mother, father and Kim pitched in to help. Rob was the exception. He stood by warily, questioning Lauren's decision. Lauren's mother kindly asked her if she was getting married quickly because she was pregnant. But after Lauren put those fears to rest, her mother enthusiastically called her minister. Reverend Corbett could accommodate them on March 3 at 7:00 p.m. The wedding date was set and it was only ten days away.

Lauren spent almost every evening with Cody, making plans of some kind. But she was worried. He was being pragmatic about the whole affair, rather than enthusiastic. He was acting as if it was a means to an end—keeping Sara safe and happy. As the day of their wedding approached, he seemed to grow more remote, and Lauren wondered if he was thinking of his wedding to Gretchen. He never talked about her.

Was he thinking about the vows he'd be making? The vows he'd made once before? Lauren knew her feelings for Cody had never diminished. Since he'd come back into her life, they'd grown stronger and stronger each day. She wanted a union with him that would last forever.

But was it too soon for him to think about that? Was it too soon for him to put his marriage to Gretchen in the past?

Yet she was afraid to ask. She didn't want to hear him say he was only marrying her because of Sara.

Four nights before the wedding, they picked up their wedding bands, then returned to Lauren's apartment to decide what things they would be moving to Cody's and what she would be sending elsewhere. As she set mugs of hot chocolate on her kitchen table, she was troubled that he hadn't kissed her or even touched her very much over the past week. Maybe she should bring it up. Maybe she should ask him why there seemed to be so much distance between them.

Before she could figure out the right way to phrase it, Cody took a mug of chocolate from her, thanked her and sat at her table. "We can use your living room suite in the basement. Eventually I want to turn that into a rec room for Sara."

"That's fine," Lauren murmured, still thinking about other things.

"We don't need another bedroom suite," he went on. "But I can store yours if you'd like."

"Kim said she'd like to have it for when Matthew gets older. They have room to keep it. What about my drafting table and desk? Could I put them in your guest bedroom and use that as an office? I often bring projects home to work on."

"I suppose you could set them up in there. If you quit working, you won't be spending much time—"

Quit working? Where had that come from? "I'm not going to stop working," she responded emphatically.

His gaze locked with hers. "You can't mother Sara and work, too."

"Why can't I? Lots of women do. My family counts on me, Cody. My landscaping skills are what makes MacMillan's different from other garden centers."

"And what are you going to do? Take Sara to work with you?"

"I thought we'd still let Kim watch her."

"No! If you're going to be her mother, then you're going to be her mother."

"I don't have to be with her twenty-four hours a day to mother her, Cody. When she goes to kindergarten next year, and then first grade—"

His jaw set with determination. "That's the point, Lauren. She needs to connect with you and spend time with you now. I never thought this would be an issue."

"It's an issue, all right, if you want me to give up what I trained to be. You never said you expected me to quit working!"

"And you didn't say you'd never consider it."

Long moments of silence vibrated in the small kitchen. Lauren could see he wasn't going to change his mind about this. Would he be so intractable on other issues? Would she have to always be the one to give in? Didn't he realize how important her work was to her?

All of Lauren's anxieties poured into her words. "My career is part of who I am, Cody. I don't go to MacMillan's every day just to pass time. I love what I do."

A hard look came into his eyes that she'd never seen there before. "If you don't want to be a mother, I never should have asked you to marry me. Sara is the reason we're getting married."

Even though she already knew the main reason they were marrying, he'd finally put it into words. With her heart hurting, she said, "We still have time to cancel the wedding."

His blue eyes were searching as he studied her. Then he nodded. "Yes, we do."

Standing, he strode out of her kitchen to her front door. "Call me when you decide what's more important to you—Sara and her well-being—or your job."

The argument had flared so quickly, they'd taken sides so steadfastly, that Lauren felt shell-shocked. Still, she knew she couldn't run after Cody like a teenager with a crush. She couldn't run after him like a desperate woman who would give up anything for marriage. She couldn't do that because she knew if she married Cody Granger, she would be giving him her heart.

Heaven help her, she was in love with him. And if he didn't have feelings for her, too...if he couldn't understand what was important to her, she couldn't marry him.

Instead of sleeping that night, Cody paced. He

wished he could take out his motorcycle, but Sara was sleeping. Never in a million years would he put his desires above his daughter's needs. Unlike Gretchen.

Maybe it had been the long labor that had made Gretchen hold back from Sara the weeks after she was born. He'd taken off as many days as he could to help his wife with their new baby, and Dolores had helped out for a few weeks after that, coming over to the house every day. But she had more than helped.

Often Gretchen had watched soap operas and gone out to lunches with friends—very long lunches. Cody had made excuses for her, diagnosing her behavior as postpartum depression. But Gretchen's attitude never really changed. Three months after Sara was born, he'd confronted his wife, insisting she either go for psychological help or act like the mother she was supposed to be. It had been one of their worst arguments. She'd shouted at him that she'd never wanted children, that Sara had ruined her figure, and now she was going to keep her daughter from ruining her life. She didn't want everything she did to re-volve around Sara, and she couldn't stand to sit at home all day, taking care of a child.

Cody had tried to decide what was best for Sara. First he'd resolved that she'd needed two parents and that he would do anything in his power to make his marriage work. Then he'd realized that if Gretchen was happy she would be a better mother. So he let her take Sara to Dolores's when she went out to lunch, when she met with the Charity Guild, when she started the fund-raiser at the hospital.

He'd poured all of his attention and caring into his

daughter when he was at home, to make sure she felt loved, to make sure Gretchen's lack of enthusiasm for being a mother didn't hurt her. But he'd worried about it constantly. Thank heaven, Sara was fine. She was bright and quick and curious. She'd connected with Lauren so quickly...

Lauren.

Did she really want to be a mother? She was so warm and so caring with Sara. But...

She wants her own career. She doesn't want to be a stay-at-home mom. She wants to put her needs before his daughter's.

Another Gretchen?

No. Her decision to marry him in itself proved that wasn't true. And if he didn't marry Lauren—

There was Dolores's threat to consider.

The ironic thing was, he *wanted* to marry Lauren. It seemed the best way to give Sara what she needed and satisfy his needs, too. He and Lauren had a sort of friendship that he'd never had with Gretchen, and he welcomed the idea of coming home to her each day and having her beside him in bed every night.

But if they couldn't bridge this gap between them...

That same night Lauren sat in her dark apartment, thinking. She'd avoided her family all day, not wanting them to see how upset she was. She hadn't been able to keep tears from coming to her eyes every time she'd thought about Sara and Cody. She *wanted* to be that little girl's mother. She wanted to be Cody's wife. But pride kept her from calling him and from trying to work out a compromise.

She asked herself why.

The answer was clear. She wasn't sure he really wanted *her*. She wasn't sure he had feelings for her or needed her for anything except keeping Dolores from filing a lawsuit.

Maybe they'd both been crazy to think a marriage like this could work.

Lauren sat in her living room most of the night, thinking about the past and the future and what she wanted. But no answer came from the heavens. No solution seemed easy. Her pride was an issue for her with Cody because of what had happened in the past.

In the morning she dressed for appointments, her first of the day in Denver. Fortunately she would be away from MacMillan's all day. If she didn't hear from Cody by tomorrow morning, the day before their wedding, she would consider their marriage plans derailed and start canceling everything.

When she returned to her office late in the day, there were no messages. She didn't hang around long enough for Rob to study her face and give her a hard time. Instead she went back to her apartment to work. But as she sat at her drafting table staring into the dark outside, rather than sketching or designing, her phone rang.

"Lauren, it's Cody."

She couldn't tell anything from his tone. "I was hoping I'd hear from you," she said honestly.

"Sara's crying. She wants you to tuck her in for the night. She fretted last night, but I managed to get her to go to sleep. Tonight that seems impossible. She's very upset, and the truth is, I don't know what to do. She wants *you*."

Lauren's heart pumped fast as she thought about Sara and the tears running down her face. But it didn't sound as if Cody wanted her to come over. Not for himself, anyway. Could his pride be standing in the way, too?

If she helped him with Sara, maybe then they could talk. One way or another they would decide whether or not they were going to get married.

"I'll be there shortly. Tell her I'm on my way."

"Thanks, Lauren."

She knew he meant it for his daughter, but what did Cody Granger feel himself?

Fifteen minutes later Lauren rang Cody's doorbell and waited. He opened the door immediately, dressed in black jeans and a faded-blue sweatshirt, looking sexy and disheveled. A lock of black hair fell over his brow, and Lauren longed to push it back. Love for him welled up inside of her, and she knew exactly why she wanted to marry him. She couldn't deny that love any longer.

As she opened the storm door and went inside, he stepped back. The tension between them was thick in the air. "Is Sara upstairs?" she asked.

"Yes. She picked out three books. I have a feeling this is going to be a long good-night. I told her to choose one, but she'll probably try to bamboozle you into two. Just wanted to warn you."

"Consider me warned," she said quietly, and then went up the stairs.

She heard him follow her, and she wished they could talk. Yet she knew they couldn't. Sara came first.

When Sara saw Lauren, she hopped out of bed and came to hug her. "I missed you," she said simply.

Lauren couldn't speak around the lump in her throat. She'd missed Sara, too, more than she'd ever thought possible. She cared about this little girl...so much.

Cody sat silently across the room as Lauren read to Sara and then, at the four-year-old's pleading, told her a story about a little bunny who was lost in the forest and had to find his way home. Weaving the tale made her concentrate and kept her mind off of Cody across the room. Sara asked questions now and then, added details of the story for herself and smiled and hugged Lauren again when she was finished.

Lauren kissed Sara's forehead and went out into the hall to wait for Cody.

When he joined her a few minutes later, they went downstairs. In the living room they stood awkwardly, gazing at each other.

"We've got to talk," he said.

"I know."

"Do you understand what I want for my daughter?" he asked in a deep voice that wasn't argumentative but rather searching.

Studying Cody, she knew Sara was everything to him. "I think I do. You want her to feel safe and secure no matter where she is, knowing she has a mother and father who care about her. I've been doing a lot of thinking about it."

His gaze never left hers. "What did you decide?"

"I don't want to give up my work. As I said, MacMillan's Garden Center depends on me."

He stiffened.

"But there's no reason why I can't work from home, is there?" she asked softly.

The lines on his brow still showed his concern. "You mean from here?"

"When I work, I need my catalogs and a phone

and a drafting table and a computer. If I could make the guest room an office..."

His stance relaxed a bit, and he took a step closer to her. "What about Sara?"

"I can work when she naps or while she's playing nearby. Fortunately my sketch pad is mobile. After you come home, I could work an hour or two more until she goes to bed. The nights you're called away, I'll have plenty to keep me busy."

He looked pensive for a few moments. "Instead of the upstairs guest room, how about if we make the solarium your office? I suppose you have meetings with clients sometimes. It would be more convenient for that."

Her heart felt light at his suggestion. "You wouldn't mind giving up the solarium?"

He came closer to her, and she felt so drawn to him that she took a deep breath as he answered, "It's just a room, Lauren. It's big enough. Sara could even have a play area in there."

For the past day or so she'd thought she'd lost the chance to marry him. But he *was* a good man, a man who was willing to compromise. "I think we can make it work, Cody. Except..." She plunged in. "I need to know you want this marriage as much as need it."

He continued to gaze down at her and finally reached out and brushed her cheek with the back of his hand. "I want this marriage, Lauren."

"For Sara's sake," she added, hoping there was more than that.

Then he said the words that made everything all right. "Not just for Sara. For me, too." Sliding his hand under her hair, he admitted, "The past two days without you, I realized how much I like having you around. I guess the idea of marrying again gave me a lot to think about.'' He nudged her closer. ''All I could think about last night was kissing you again.''

As his lips came down on hers, there was no doubt that he *wanted* to kiss her. It was not a duty kiss. It was demanding and possessive and everything Lauren wanted from Cody. It took her to a place where dreams could come true, and she could believe their marriage would succeed. In his arms she became a real woman who wanted to learn everything he had to teach.

They ended up on the sofa, the kiss taking them places they hadn't been before. She lay back against a pillow, and he came down on top of her. ''I want you, Lauren.''

She didn't doubt the sincerity of his words or the blaze of desire in his eyes. Maybe everything was going to be all right. Maybe in time he would come to love her the way she loved him.

As he kissed her again, his hand went to her breast and she arched into it, remembering that night with him in his car so long ago. Remembering his touch. He slipped his hand under her sweater and it came to rest on her breast. His skin was hot on hers, the pad of his thumb rough as he edged the top of her bra. She moaned into the kiss. How she loved his touch; how she loved his weight on her. How she loved Cody.

The hard ridge of his arousal was exciting. Though she was inexperienced, she knew moving against him would give him pleasure. She did that and heard him groan, pleasing herself as well as pleasing him.

''I want to undress you, Lauren.''

She wanted that. She wanted to be rid of the barriers between them. Yet suddenly she realized...

Pulling away from the kiss, she caught her breath and murmured, "Cody, I'm still a virgin."

He stilled, and she could see the astonishment in his eyes. "You're serious?"

She nodded.

"You must be the last one," he murmured with a crooked smile.

His teasing rankled. "I don't know if I'm the last one. I just know——" She stopped.

"What do you know?" he asked gently.

"I just know I was waiting. For the right time and the right place and the right man."

Cody gazed down at her and searched her face, then he levered himself up. "I think we'd better catch our breath."

He didn't seem angry, yet he'd stopped. She slid her legs to the floor, trying to slow her pulse, taking a deep breath.

With a glance at her he said, "If you're waiting for the right place and the right time, I'm not sure this is it." His eyes caught hers then and held. "I won't rush you into anything. Not now. Not after we're married. You have to be ready, and you have to say the word."

How could Cody turn on and off his desire so easily? How could he stop, when all she wanted was to become one with him? The fact that he *could* made her think——

Maybe he didn't desire her as much as she desired him.

Maybe it would be better if they waited until after the wedding ceremony...when they were truly man and wife. Then she could tell him she wanted him. Then she could tell him she was ready.

On Wednesday night she would be Mrs. Cody Granger. Then she'd have the husband and the life she'd always wanted.

Chapter Six

An hour before her wedding, Lauren stood in the parlor of her minister's house, letting her friend Eve Coleburn fasten the small buttons at the back of her gown. Although Kim was going to be Lauren's matron of honor, she wouldn't be arriving until shortly before the ceremony. Lauren had asked Eve to be in her wedding also because they had become close friends over the past year since Eve had moved to Denver and married Hunter Coleburn.

Fastening the last button, Eve said, "I just love your dress. It's so elegant."

Lauren ran her hands over the slim skirt of the satin-and-lace gown with its delicate appliqués, hoping it made her look as beautiful as she felt in it. When Eve attached the train, it flowed softly around her. She wanted to be beautiful for Cody today. She wanted him to look at her and...

Forget Gretchen?

Forget he was marrying her for the sake of his daughter?

When Eve took Lauren's sheer tulle veil from the high-backed wing chair, Lauren studied her. She'd arranged her black hair in a French twist and, in a deep green velvet gown, looked as beautiful as a bride herself. No one could ever tell she'd had a baby six weeks ago. She was as slim as she'd been before her pregnancy.

Lifting the headpiece to her friend's hair, Eve searched Lauren's face. "What's wrong, Lauren?"

She and Eve hadn't known each other long, but they'd come to know each other pretty well. "Just jitters, I guess."

"I think it's more than jitters. When you came over to the house a few weeks ago, you didn't even tell me you were dating someone. Then suddenly last week you asked me to be in your wedding. What's going on?"

Lauren hadn't confided in anyone the reason she was marrying Cody, or rather the reason he'd asked her to marry him. She didn't want her parents to worry. She didn't want Rob to criticize, and she wasn't sure how Kim would react to the idea of a marriage of convenience.

Now, with her friend looking at her so compassionately, the words came tumbling out. "Cody and I are getting married for the sake of his daughter, so his mother-in-law doesn't sue for custody."

Eve didn't react with the shock that Lauren expected. "Is his daughter the only reason you're getting married?"

"No. We knew each other in high school, and I've always been...very attracted to Cody. More than that really. I do love him.'' Repositioning her train, Lauren avoided Eve's gaze.

"But…?" Eve prompted, her Southern accent softening her question.

Finally Lauren expressed her worst fear. "But I'm not sure he has any feelings for me. I think he's attracted to me, but I'm not sure it goes any deeper than that." Then she lifted her eyes to her friend's. "You must think I'm crazy to do this."

"No, I don't think you're crazy," Eve assured her gently. "I loved Hunter when I married him, but I wasn't sure he loved me."

"Are you serious?" Lauren asked. Anyone who saw Eve and Hunter together could practically touch the aura of love that surrounded them.

"Very serious. We married because my father's will stipulated that if I didn't marry within a year I'd lose my inheritance."

"You were strangers?"

"Oh, no. I'd fallen in love with Hunter five years before. But for lots of reasons I'd refused his marriage proposal. It took us a long while to find our way back to each other, and it didn't happen until after we were married."

Lauren could remember the night that Eve had been so upset not so long after their friendship had begun, the night she'd left their dinner early to go home to Hunter. "But you're happy now?"

"I've never been happier. And since Carly Ann was born, I feel so fulfilled it's hard to explain sometimes."

There was a radiant glow around Eve that had come with motherhood. "I can only imagine how it would feel to have a baby. I can't wait to mother

PLAY "LUCKY 7" AND GET
THREE FREE GIFTS!

HOW TO PLAY:

1. With a coin, carefully scratch off the silver box at the right. Then check the claim chart see what we have for you — **2 FREE BOOKS** and a gift — **ALL YOURS! ALL FREE!**

2. Send back this card and you'll receive two brand-new Silhouette Romance® novels. The books have a cover price of $3.50 each in the U.S. and $3.99 each in Canada, but they a yours to keep absolutely free.

3. There's no catch. You're under obligation to buy anything. W charge nothing — ZERO — your first shipment. And you do have to make any minimum numb of purchases — not even one!

4. The fact is thousands of readers enjoy receiving their books by mail from the Silhoue Reader Service.™ They enjoy the convenience of home delivery... they like getting the be new novels at discount prices, BEFORE they're available in stores...and they love their *He to Heart* newsletter featuring author news, horoscopes, recipes, book reviews and much mo

5. We hope that after receiving your free books you'll want to remain a subscriber. B the choice is yours — to continue or cancel, any time at all! So why not take us up on o invitation, with no risk of any kind. You'll be glad you did!

YOURS FREE!

PLAY LUCKY 7 FOR THIS EXCITING FREE GIFT!

THIS SURPRISE MYSTERY GIFT COULD BE YOURS FREE WHEN YOU PLAY

LUCKY 7!

The Silhouette Reader Service™ — Here's how it works:

Accepting your 2 free books and gift places you under no obligation to buy anything. You may keep the books and gift and return the shipping statement marked "cancel." If you do not cancel, about a month later we'll send you 6 additional novels and bill you just $2.90 each in the U.S., or $3.25 each in Canada, plus 25¢ shipping & handling per book and applicable taxes if any.* That's the complete price and — compared to cover prices of $3.50 each in the U.S. and $3.99 each in Canada — it's quite a bargain! You may cancel at any time, but if you choose to continue, every month we'll send you 6 more books, which you may either purchase at the discount price or return to us and cancel your subscription.

*Terms and prices subject to change without notice. Sales tax applicable in N.Y. Canadian residents will be charged applicable provincial taxes and GST.

BUSINESS REPLY MAIL

FIRST-CLASS MAIL   PERMIT NO. 717   BUFFALO, NY

POSTAGE WILL BE PAID BY ADDRESSEE

SILHOUETTE READER SERVICE
3010 WALDEN AVE
PO BOX 1867
BUFFALO NY 14240-9952

NO POSTAGE
NECESSARY
IF MAILED
IN THE
UNITED STATES

Sara—really mother her. Maybe someday Cody and I will have a child. We haven't talked about it. I just wish..."

"What do you wish?"

"That Cody could see today as a wonderful beginning, rather than as a bargain we made."

Eve's blue eyes were sparkling clear and direct. "Maybe he does see it that way. But if you have doubts, Lauren, maybe you shouldn't do this."

As she had for the past ten days, she examined her decision again. Then she said, "When I think about marrying Cody, I'm afraid. But when I think about *not* marrying Cody—" She stopped. "It's worth the risk, Eve. Deep in my heart, I know it is."

"Then let's get you ready to meet your groom," Eve suggested with an understanding smile.

It wasn't long until Kim arrived and then Lauren's parents. With tears in her eyes, Lauren's mother gave her a hug. Her soft, gray hair curled around her face as she gazed at her daughter. "I hope you and Cody can find the happiness that your father and I have always found together."

Her dad, whose brown hair was balding on the top of his head, whose waistline was thicker than it had been in years, smiled at his daughter and offered her his arm. "Can I escort you to your wedding?"

With tears suspended in her throat, Lauren looped her arm into her father's and walked with him from the minister's house the short distance to the church. As they entered the vestibule, music began playing, and Kim and Eve took their places in the doorway. When Rob escorted Lauren's mother up the aisle, Lauren saw that Dolores was already seated with Sara beside her.

Then everything started happening quickly. On a cue from the minister, who was now standing at the altar, Eve and then Kim began walking down the aisle. Lauren glimpsed Cody and Eli Hastings as they joined the minister in the front of the church. Cody looked about ten feet tall in his tuxedo. The black and white, his handsome face, the strength and confidence that always seemed to emanate from him made him appear larger than life to her. A few minutes later she was standing in the doorway with her father, and the organ music changed. Everyone in the church knew the bride was on her way.

When Cody saw Lauren, the world seemed to stop for a moment. He thought she'd never looked more beautiful, and he realized he wanted her in the way he hadn't wanted a woman in a very long time. Yet he knew he would have to go slowly. She was a virgin. And this marriage was different from most. It was an agreement. A safeguard. An attempt to build more from a renewed friendship that had begun so long ago.

This day couldn't help but bring back another memory. He'd been so hopeful when he'd married Gretchen, so sure he'd found everything he'd wanted. Unfortunately, marriage didn't guarantee happiness.

He'd expected everything from Gretchen. Commitment. Support. Most of all an intimacy that began in bed and should have grown in the nurturing of their daughter together. But Gretchen's support of his career had been for her own gain. Her commitment had been to their lifestyle, not their marriage. Intimacy in bed had dwindled to duty until pride had caused him to deny his needs. He'd poured his pas-

sion into work and raising their daughter, while
Gretchen had poured her passion into causes that had
made her look good in the community.

No, marriage wouldn't guarantee happiness, but it
would keep his daughter with him. That was what
was most important to him now.

After Lauren handed her bouquet to Kim, Cody
took her hand and she stepped up beside him. He
listened to the minister's words, allowing them to
flow over him without touching him. If he went into
this marriage without expectations, he wouldn't be
disappointed. If he looked on Lauren as a helpmate
and a friend, they could build a good life. He
wouldn't let himself hope for the moon. He and Lauren would concentrate on Sara's welfare, and that
would be their common ground.

When it came time to say his vows, Cody did so
with more determination than feeling. As Lauren repeated the same words, her voice caught. Cody wondered if she was having second thoughts, if she was
worried about tonight, if she'd forgiven him for hurting her so long ago. But then her voice became
strong again, and she finished her promises.

They exchanged wedding bands, plain gold ones.
Gretchen had insisted on a diamond band, and since
they'd waited so long to get married, he'd bought
her one, wanting to make her happy, wanting to give
her everything he could. Yet he hadn't been able to
give enough. He hadn't been able to *be* enough.
They'd ended up living together but not sharing,
sleeping together but not being truly intimate.

The final blessing took only a few moments. On
the instructions of the minister Cody kissed Lauren,

claiming her with a fervor that disconcerted him and made him end the kiss hastily.

After the minister introduced them to their friends and family as husband and wife, they walked down the steps. When Sara ran from the pew into the aisle, Cody caught her up into his arms, and Lauren hugged his daughter as if she really wanted to. The three of them walked down the white runner to the vestibule together and stopped in the back of the church.

"Is Lauren coming home with us now, Daddy?" Sara asked.

Cody glanced at Lauren and then back at his daughter. He'd told Sara this morning that the three of them were going to be a family and live together. Answering her now, he said, "We're going to a party and then we'll all go home together."

With a fanfare of music coming from the piano at the Briarwood Club, Lauren and Cody stepped under the wedding arch into a roomful of guests. Everyone applauded them, and Lauren knew she had to smile. Their wedding had been beautiful...everything she could have imagined. Except the groom wasn't in love with her. Cody had treated the wedding as a ritual, rather than a spiritual union that could join their hearts and lives. Still, at this moment, as they stood before family and friends, she decided that love could make a difference. If she could show Cody she was worthy of his love, maybe it would come. Maybe he could put his life with Gretchen in the past.

Cody's hand settled in the small of Lauren's back

as he guided her to the head table. But Sara came running over to them.

"Are you having fun with Grammy?" Lauren asked, crouching down to Sara's level.

"I want to sit with you."

"We're sitting at a table just for big people," Cody explained to his daughter.

At the little girl's frown and the quiver of her lip, Lauren stroked her hair. "I'll tell you what. If you stay with Grammy now, you can come and sit with us after we cut the cake and have dessert with us. How does that sound?"

Sara thought about it for a few moments and then nodded. "Okay. I'll go tell Grammy."

"You're sure you don't mind?" Cody asked when Sara ran off.

"I don't mind. It's a special day for her, too."

"You're going to be a very good mother," he said, as if what had just happened had reassured him.

"I hope so."

The warm lights in Cody's eyes enveloped her like a reassuring cloak. If she did everything in her power to show Cody she could be a good mother, maybe he would let his guard down...maybe he'd let himself feel more than friendship for her.

The reception went smoothly. After Cody and Lauren cut the cake, he carefully fed her a piece. His thumb touched her bottom lip, and she shivered from the excitement of knowing he was her husband. When she fed him his piece, he caught her fingers between his lips and didn't pull back for a long moment.

Gazing into his eyes, she saw desire, and thought, *At least this is a starting place.*

The maître d' wedged a chair in beside Cody so Sara could sit there to eat her cake. She thoroughly enjoyed it, smudging icing all over her upper lip. Lauren happened to glance at Dolores, who was sitting at a table with the MacMillan family, but wasn't talking to any of them. Her gaze focused on Sara, and Lauren realized just how alone Dolores DeWitt was.

Leaning toward her new husband, Lauren asked, "Does Dolores go out much? I mean with men."

Cody shook his head. "Not that I know of. She talks often about lunches with women in her bridge club, but she never talks about dating."

"I don't think she believes you're not a fit father or that your hours are too long. I think she's lonely, and Sara puts meaning in her life."

"Maybe that *is* the reason she wants to spend time with her, but I won't let her spoil Sara. I won't let her turn her into a little princess—" He stopped.

"Don't you think all grandparents spoil their grandchildren? It might just be part of being a grandparent."

His jaw set until finally he asked, "Do you think I should let Dolores buy Sara whatever she wants?"

"Of course not. But maybe if we give her a little latitude, as well as a little more time with Sara, she'll realize she doesn't have to hold on quite so tightly."

Cody shook his head. "Don't underestimate Dolores. I think she's the type of woman who when given an inch will take a yard."

Obviously Cody knew his mother-in-law better than Lauren did. But she still believed the woman was lonely, and that was a big part of the problem.

Lauren had just finished her cake when the maître

d' came to them. He said, "It's time for the first dance. Are you ready?"

Cody arched his brows at Lauren, and she nodded. When Sara was safely back in Dolores's care, Cody took Lauren into his arms on the dance floor. The pianist played a romantic ballad, and Lauren looked up at her new husband.

"Was today everything you wanted it to be?" he asked.

"Our wedding turned out beautifully," she responded.

There were a few awkward moments of silence until he suggested, "Maybe we can get away for a few days in April. Eli and I are thinking about bringing another doctor into the practice."

"I'd like that."

Aware of everyone's eyes on them, Lauren and Cody's dance was more perfunctory than intimate. For the next number, the wedding party joined them on the dance floor, and Eli was partnered with Dolores.

Halfway through the dance, he and Dolores stopped beside Cody and Lauren. "Time for me to dance with the new bride," Eli said with a grin.

Eli Hastings had twinkling green eyes, gray hair swept back from a receding hairline, and a smile capable of comforting any patient. As Eli danced Lauren away from Cody and Dolores, he smiled down at her. "It's about time I get a moment alone with you. I want to tell you how pleased I am to see you and Cody together. That boy needs a good woman in his life."

"You mean because of Sara?"

"No, I don't. Maybe he needs a mother for Sara, but he needs somebody to share his life even more."

Lauren suspected Eli knew Cody better than anyone else. "Why do you think so?"

"Cody had it rough, growing up. Not much caring there. So there were consequences. He thinks he can tackle the world on his own. Since he's been back here, I see the results of that. He works and he takes care of Sara. He needs more than responsibility in his life, and I suppose he's marrying you because you've shown him that."

How Lauren wished Eli was right. Having known Eli for years herself, and trusting him, she asked, "Does Cody ever talk about his first wife?"

Eli's gaze was troubled. "No, he doesn't. I thought maybe he had with you."

"Not yet."

"Give him time, Lauren."

She could do that. They had a lifetime together. She just couldn't push for too much, too fast.

Lauren waited for Cody in the master bedroom. It was almost eleven-thirty. She'd forgotten about the buttons down the back of her dress, and she couldn't get out of it without some help. Sara had been almost asleep during the drive home. Cody had carried her inside, straight up to her bedroom, telling Lauren he would put his daughter to bed if she wanted to get out of her wedding gown.

But she couldn't get out of it. She'd detached her train and unpinned the headdress with its veil and laid it on a corner of the long dresser. When she went to the closet, it seemed strange to see her clothes in a different place. They'd moved all of her things over yesterday. She took out the nightgown and robe that she'd bought especially for tonight. They were pale pink satin, and more feminine than anything she'd ever purchased.

When the door to the bedroom opened, she turned to face Cody. He looked surprised to see her still in her wedding gown.

"I can't undo the buttons on the back." Her voice was a bit shaky. What would he expect tonight? Could she please him?

Shrugging out of his tuxedo jacket, he laid it over the bedroom chair. "Turn around, and I'll see what I can do."

She faced away from him, holding her breath. When his fingers unfastened the first button and brushed against her skin, she could feel a tremor ripple through her. The buttons were tiny, and it seemed to take forever for him to unfasten each one. Her sleeves slipped down her shoulders, and she held up the bodice of the dress until he finished.

There was silence in the room. Finally he said, "All done. If you'd like to use the bathroom first, feel free."

She glanced at him over her shoulder and gave him a smile. "I won't be long." Gathering up her robe and gown, she went into the bathroom, her heart pounding as she anticipated her first night in bed with her husband.

Fifteen minutes later she entered the bedroom with her wedding gown in hand, freshly showered, her robe belted with its pink satin ribbon. When she saw Cody, she froze. He was bare to the waist, and she couldn't tear her gaze from his chest. Brown, curling hair formed an arrow down the middle to below the waistband of the tuxedo trousers. Swallowing hard, she looked away, picking up the hanger from her wedding dress and concentrating on arranging it. Cody went into the bathroom, and a few moments later she heard the shower running.

Only one dim light glowed on his side of the bed. After she hung her wedding gown in the walk-in closet, she took off her robe and slipped under the covers, waiting for Cody, wondering if he would wear anything to bed.

It seemed like forever until he returned. The bed was a king-size one, and as he sat on his side, she could hardly feel the movement. He switched off the light, and she knew he was close in the darkness but not close enough to touch.

"I guess Sara fell right back to sleep," she said to make conversation.

"She could hardly keep her eyes open. She's not used to being up this late."

Silence pulsed between them.

"Lauren, as I told you, I'm not going to rush you into anything. I know all of this happened quickly, and we both need time to absorb it."

She didn't know if he was just being considerate, or if this wedding night reminded him too much of another. Truth be told, she wasn't confident enough to make the first move. So she simply responded, "Thank you, Cody."

"Eli is covering my rounds at the hospital tomorrow morning. So I thought we could all go out to breakfast together and get Sara used to us being a family."

"That sounds like a good idea."

Silence pervaded the room once more...until Cody said, "Sweet dreams, Lauren."

"Good night, Cody." She knew her dreams would be sweet...because they would be of him.

The clear cold felt good to Cody as he and Barry Sentz approached Cody's front door on Saturday afternoon. As usual, they'd played basketball, working off whatever problems had mounted up over the week. Today Cody had played harder than ever. The past two nights he'd lain beside Lauren in their bed, wanting her. He'd been waiting for some signal from her...some signal that she was ready.

But she hadn't given him one.

He wouldn't push her. But whenever he was near her, he was in turmoil, and he couldn't figure out why. Maybe it was because he didn't want to repeat past mistakes. He wasn't even sure what they were, what had caused the distance between him and Gretchen...what had caused their marriage to flounder. Had Gretchen's attitude toward mothering and his worry for Sara started the resentment that had grown between them? Or had something been lacking all along? He still wasn't sure.

As Cody pushed open his front door, Barry carried in a box from his car. He hadn't been able to come to Cody's wedding because he'd been out of town. But he'd bought them a wedding present and wanted to give it to Lauren.

As they entered the kitchen, Cody saw her standing at the sink, slicing apples into a dish. She was wearing denim overalls with a white-and-red checkered blouse. Her hair was tied up in a ponytail, and she'd never looked cuter. Cody felt the heat of desire flash through him, and he knew lying beside her another night without touching her, without kissing her and making her his, would be torture.

Glancing over her shoulder, she saw them, then rinsed her hands and dried them. ''Hi,'' she said.

Barry set the package on the table and stepped forward, his hand extended. ''Barry Sentz. I don't know if you remember me.''

''Sure, I do. You were in Cody's class.''

''I'm sorry I couldn't make it to the wedding, so I wanted to drop this off. I hope you don't have one.'' He looked around the kitchen.

''I'll open it and find out,'' she said with another smile. Tearing off the bow, she carefully unfastened the paper and revealed a cappuccino machine. She looked pleased. ''Thanks, Barry. We don't have one.''

The lawyer glanced from her to Cody. ''You know, I never thought you two would end up together when I advised Cody to find a wife. Not after the prom fiasco. But I guess you're the type who forgives and forgets.''

Lauren looked up at Barry, her eyes wide, as she realized once more he'd witnessed and obviously remembered exactly what had happened between her and Cody when they were teenagers. ''Holding on to the past doesn't do anyone any good,'' she murmured.

Cody knew Lauren meant what she said, but he also heard something else in her voice, something that told him that the hurt wasn't altogether gone. Maybe it was time they really talked about it.

He said to Barry, ''Thanks for the present.''

There was tension in the kitchen that hadn't been

there before, and Barry seemed to notice it. "Well, I'd better be going. I've got to shower, then go back to the office for a while. It was nice to see you again, Lauren."

"You, too," she said, but her smile was weak now.

"I can see myself out, I've done it often enough. I'll call you, Cody, to set up the next game."

Suddenly Cody and Lauren were alone in the kitchen, staring at each other, totally mindful of the past that Barry had resurrected.

After Cody heard the front door close, he shrugged out of his warm-up jacket and threw it over the back of a chair. "Is Sara napping?"

Lauren just nodded and would have turned away to go back to what she'd been doing, but he caught her arm. "Have you really let go of the past?"

She faced him, her eyes troubled. "I've tried. We were both young, and I had lots of illusions. I know you wouldn't have dated me in high school if you hadn't been on the rebound."

Unfortunately, he couldn't tell her she was wrong. He couldn't tell her that her friendliness and interest back then had been more than a balm for his bruised ego. Yet he'd liked her, too. And he realized something else. "If Gretchen and I hadn't gotten back together, you and I might have had a chance."

"But you *did* get back together with Gretchen. Do you realize that's the first you've mentioned her name to me? I don't even know how she died. You can talk to me about it. I'll understand."

His marriage to Gretchen had been lonely and painful, and when she died, he'd had so many regrets. "She died in an automobile accident. She was driving home from a meeting, late one night. The roads were icy and she skidded—'' He broke off. ''I don't talk about it because there's no need to.''

Lauren studied him intently. ''Do you talk to Sara about her mother?''

''Yes, when she asks...or when we look at the photo albums together. But she doesn't ask often. I concentrate on *her* because she's my life now.''

''I know she is.'' Lauren's tone was serious. Moving away from him, she said, ''I think I'll go upstairs and see if she's awake. She might want to watch me make apple cobbler.''

Cody longed to take Lauren into his arms...to forget all about his marriage to Gretchen...to act like a new bridegroom. But he was sweaty from the game, and he didn't know what Lauren wanted. He also didn't know if she'd truly forgiven him for what had happened thirteen years ago. He had to give her more time.

It was a good thing he was a patient man.

Chapter Seven

On Sunday afternoon Cody hefted a silver maple onto the bed of a pickup truck. Spring and Easter were coming. Lauren's family was preparing the garden center and needed her to help out today. He'd decided to come along, too. He wanted to get to know Lauren's family better.

Kim was inside the showroom with Lindsey, Sara and Matt, helping the kids do puzzles. Lauren's mom was manning the cashier's desk, while Rob and Lauren's dad worked outside. They all had embraced Sara as if she had always been a member of their family. The dynamics of the MacMillan family intrigued Cody. They all worked together so peaceably and didn't think twice about helping each other.

But for the past twenty minutes, while Cody had loaded trees onto the truck, he'd kept one eye on Lauren. She was standing outside the showroom door, involved in a conversation with a good-looking middle-aged man.

A clipboard in hand, Rob came over to the truck. "Thanks for helping out today, Cody. I didn't think doctors would know how to do heavy labor."

Rob hadn't been overly friendly since Cody had returned to Birch Creek. Even at the wedding he'd kept his distance. "I worked construction jobs during summers when I was in college. I'm no stranger to manual labor."

Leaning casually against the side of the pickup, Rob asked, "Are you on call today?"

"Yep, I'm covering for Eli. But so far, so good."

"I guess your practice is the reason you and Lauren didn't take a honeymoon."

Lauren's brother was fishing. "One of the reasons," Cody said. "Sara is another. She and Lauren are getting to know each other, and we thought it might be better if we wait to go away." It all sounded so reasonable. If they *had* gone away on a honeymoon, maybe they would have consummated their marriage by now.

As Cody glanced over at Lauren again, he saw the man she was with touch her elbow in a familiar gesture. "Who is that guy?" Cody asked Rob.

Rob looked in the direction of Cody's gaze. "Craig Davis. He's an architect with Davis, Willis and Green. Lauren's worked with him on a couple of projects. In fact, I think she just put a bid in to landscape the grounds of an office building he designed. If she gets that contract, there will be more like it."

Cody's mind wasn't on the work Lauren would be doing. "Is he married?"

"Divorced. Why?"

"Because he's looking at Lauren as if—" Cody stopped abruptly.

Rob just arched his brows. "As if...?"

"As if he has more on his mind than work," Cody muttered.

"You can always go over there and break it up," Rob suggested with a sly smile.

"Maybe I'll do just that." Cody jumped off the back of the pickup. "Everything you asked for is loaded on the truck."

"Thanks. I'll take it from here. Uh, Cody...you should probably know that Lauren's gone out with Craig several times. Before you came back to Birch Creek, she was talking about dating him more seriously."

Cody had gotten the impression that Lauren didn't date much. But just because she was a virgin didn't mean she didn't go out. He disliked the idea of her dating another man. He disliked the idea of her being so friendly with one, too.

Crossing quickly to the showroom, Cody approached Lauren.

Seeing him, she smiled. That smile was worth a million bucks, and she didn't even know it. "Sara's still doing puzzles," she said as if she thought he might be concerned about his daughter.

When they'd first arrived, Lauren had taken Sara to the greenhouses with her. Sara had been happy helping Lauren water plants and line up pots on skids.

"Sara likes playing with Lindsey and Matt." Cody was much more concerned about Lauren's relationship with Craig Davis. He turned to the man. "I don't think we've met."

Lauren blushed slightly. "Craig, this is my husband, Cody Granger. Cody, Craig Davis. Craig's an architect."

Cody nodded and so did Craig. Neither extended a hand.

Politely Craig said, "Congratulations on your wedding. You're a lucky man. Lauren's a talented lady."

"Yes, she is." Cody had the strongest desire to scoop Lauren into his arms and carry her away. But instead of that he rested his hand on her shoulder. "And I need to talk to her for a few minutes. Do you mind?"

Craig looked discomfited but shook his head. "No, of course not. I have to be going, anyway. Lauren, I'll see you next month, if not before."

"Right," she responded.

As soon as Craig Davis walked away, Cody turned to Lauren. "Are you two working on a project together?" He tried to keep his question nonchalant.

"He's working up house plans for a new client, and he wants my opinion on the landscaping."

"I see. Will you be meeting at his office?"

"Perhaps. Or at the house. Unless you would rather I meet him here."

"No, of course not. That's why I gave you the solarium. I knew you'd have clients coming in."

After studying him, she said, "But...?"

Lauren was a perceptive woman. He might as well tell her what was on his mind. "Rob said you dated Craig Davis."

She looked surprised. "We went to dinner a few times."

"That's all? You had dinner?"

Her cheeks flushed slightly. "Yes."

"Rob also said you were thinking about getting more serious about him."

Slipping one hand into the pocket of her jacket, she answered, "Once I thought that. But then he was out of town on business a lot, and I was busy here. So it never developed into anything more."

As she tilted her head, the sun caught the blond strands in her hair and spun them into gold. She looked so lovely, Cody's breath almost caught in his chest, and the rush of desire that swept through him startled even him.

"I think he would like more than a professional relationship with you." His voice came out deep and husky as he thought about what another man wanting Lauren would mean.

"He knows all we can have is a professional relationship. I'm married to you now."

"A wedding band doesn't stop some men."

"Or some women?" she asked, gazing up at him speculatively. "Don't you trust me, Cody?"

Trust. That was one of those words that was much more complicated than the spelling of it. "We haven't had much time to build trust. Do *you* trust *me?*"

In her eyes he could almost see her thoughts. He'd asked her to the prom and then kissed Gretchen. They'd been so young then, and they were adults now. But he was concerned Lauren's trust in him had been shaken.

Her words proved it had been. "As you said, Cody, trust takes time to build."

After an awkward silence, she moved a few steps

away. "I think I'll take Sara and Lindsey and show them the lilies. I need to inventory them."

As she turned, Cody wanted to stop her, and yet he had no reason to. He was suddenly very anxious to teach his wife that she could trust him. But he wasn't sure how to do that. Just as he wasn't sure if he could ever completely trust or depend on someone else himself. Gretchen had made a huge hole in is ability to do either. It was safer to be self-sufficient...safer not to confide...safer not to feel too much.

It was almost four o'clock when Cody saw Dolores's car pull into the nursery's parking lot. He was helping to load a flat of pansies into a customer's van. When Dolores saw him, she just gaped. "What are you doing?"

"I'm pitching in," he said lightly. "How did you know where to find me?"

"I didn't. You never tell me where you're going to be. But I thought maybe Lauren would be here, and she and I could have a little talk."

"About?" he asked suspiciously.

"Just women talk. Is Sara here, too?"

"She's with Lauren...in the greenhouse."

"Well, I hope she's not running wild. She could hurt herself in a place like this."

"Lauren's very careful with Sara, Dolores. She wouldn't let her get hurt." Suddenly anger gripped him when he thought about all the times Gretchen had left Sara with Dolores. And before he could stop the words, they poured out. "Unlike your daughter, Lauren likes caring for Sara. She likes playing with her. She's going to be a very *good* mother."

When Dolores's face paled, he felt guilty for his

blunt honesty. He and Dolores had never talked about Gretchen's shortcomings, because Dolores didn't want to believe they existed. But they both knew better. He hadn't realized the resentment was still lingering. But it was, and somehow he had to get rid of it.

He clasped his former mother-in-law's arm. "I didn't mean for it to come out like that."

She pulled away. "Yes, you did. I imagine there are lots of things you haven't said that you'd like to say. But they'll just have to wait. I want to spend time with my granddaughter." Cutting off any further discussion, she headed for the greenhouses.

Fifteen minutes later he spotted Dolores with Kim by the showroom door and decided to make peace with her. That was the only way Sara would be happy.

But as he approached the women, he heard Kim say, "I think they're very happy. Lauren said something about a honeymoon in April."

Dolores didn't even blink as Cody stepped up beside her. He imagined she was pumping Kim for information about his relationship with Lauren because she still didn't believe it was genuine. "If you want to know anything about my marriage, Dolores, ask me," he said firmly.

But Dolores didn't have a chance to ask any more questions because Sara came running up to them with a small potted lily in her hands. She gave it to her grandmother. "This is for you. Lauren said you can have it."

Dolores saw Lauren walking toward her, took the lily and then stooped to hug her granddaughter. Her voice was faint when she said, "Thank you, honey."

While granddaughter and grandmother hugged, Lauren pulled Cody aside. "Why don't we ask Dolores to come over for dinner tonight? I can make barbecued hamburger or something else that's easy."

"I found her pumping Kim for information. Are you sure you want to invite her?"

Lauren's voice was low. "I think she's just lonely. She wants to be part of a family and doesn't have any family to be part of. Maybe if we include her in ours, she'll realize we're not going to keep Sara away from her."

"I don't want Sara adopting her set of values."

"Cody, Sara's going to grow up with *our* influence. What we do every day with her is what matters. And if we see Dolores is bending her in a direction we don't want her to go, we'll do something about it. But I don't think we have to worry about that yet."

His wife was a sweet woman on the inside as well as the outside. "You're probably the kindest woman I know," he said sincerely.

As always when he paid her a compliment, Lauren's face turned rosy. "Thanks. But I'm just looking out for Sara's good and ours, too. If we make Dolores our friend, she won't be an enemy. I'll tell her we're not having anything fancy, but she's welcome to join us."

When Lauren asked Dolores to join them for supper, Cody realized again how amazing Lauren was, how glad he was he was married to her and going to build a life with her. And maybe tonight...

Maybe tonight they'd become husband and wife in reality as well as on paper.

* * *

Leaving her robe on the hook in the bathroom, Lauren went into the bedroom wearing the nightgown she'd bought for her wedding night. When Cody had seen her with Craig today, there had been a look in his eyes that had been different. She wasn't sure what it was, but it excited her and gave her hope that he desired her in the way a man in love desires a woman.

She stopped when she saw him. He was sitting in the bedroom chair in his sleeping shorts, his legs propped on the bed while he read a medical journal. Everything about him was strong and hard and muscled. Just looking at him made her stomach tipsy.

When he heard her come into the room, he looked up. His gaze lingered on the spaghetti straps of her gown, the satin material clinging to her breasts and falling over the swell of her hips to her ankles.

He shifted his legs from the bed, and she was suddenly very nervous. "I think supper went pretty well, don't you?" she asked.

It took him a moment to answer. "I guess. I'm not sure Dolores is used to eating sloppy Joes."

Lauren laughed. "I've never seen anyone take so long to eat a sandwich. She must have wiped her fingers on her napkin after every bite."

"She's a perfect lady," Cody admitted.

Then they both looked at each other and burst into laughter.

"We might be able to get her to let her hair down until we're done with her. I think I'll invite her to dinner with my parents and ask Eli to come over. What do you think?"

"Eli and Dolores?" Cody looked incredulous.

"I think they'd find each other very interesting."

Cody cocked his head and studied her. "The MacMillans are quite a family, aren't they?"

"I don't know what you mean."

Standing, he laid the medical journal on the corner of the bed and came toward her. "I've never seen a family work together the way you do."

As he drew closer, his bare chest was within reach, and she swallowed hard. "We love each other, Cody, and we help out when we're needed."

"You're lucky to have grown up the way you did, respecting your parents and everything about the way they live their lives."

"Didn't you respect your parents?" She'd heard rumors about Cody's father, but she wanted to hear the truth from him.

"My father didn't give me anything *to* respect. He was in and out of jail, always looking for the closest drink and the nearest poker game. I remember the police coming in the middle of the night to arrest him for fencing stolen goods. He was out on parole when he died from cirrhosis."

The sad look in Cody's eyes tore at her heart as she imagined what he'd gone through. "That must have been hard on you."

"What was hard was watching my mother work her fingers to the bone in minimum-wage jobs that hardly kept a roof over our heads. When I asked her why she didn't divorce my dad, she said she loved him. But he didn't love her. He couldn't have. Not the way he yelled at her. Not the way he drank. Not the way he left for weeks at a time. Not the way he got himself into one bad situation after another."

Cody's expression was grim. "She died of pneumonia when I was in college, because she couldn't afford to go to the doctor. Eli would have treated her without payment, but she was too proud."

"I'm sorry, Cody. I'm sorry you didn't have parents like mine or a brother and sister to share with."

"I don't usually talk about it," he said in a low voice as if he was surprised he'd spoken of it now.

"I'm glad you told me. I'm glad you trusted me enough to tell me." She believed that was a huge step for him and probably one for her, too. It brought them closer together.

As if reading her mind, Cody stepped forward and slid his hand under her hair. He gazed into her eyes for a few long moments. When his head bent to hers, she knew she had waited all her life for this moment...for this man.

He angled his lips over hers, opening his mouth, waiting for her to open hers.

Lauren wasn't sure how to give him what he wanted. Could she please him? Could she bind him to her with desire rather than love? Would the love follow? All she had was hope. And she hung on to that the same way she hung on to Cody.

When she opened her mouth to him, he possessively took command, seducing her with his scent and taste and texture. His skin was taut and hot under her fingers as she gripped his shoulders and explored the muscles there. His hands slipped from her hair, slid down her back, caressing it in long strokes that brought her closer to him.

She didn't understand the tightening coil of desire inside of her. She knew it was caused by her body, pressed against his, his hard arousal satisfying some primitive need as she longed to discard her nightgown. She had no idea how it would feel to be joined to Cody, but the excitement tingling in every part of her told her it could be wonderful and joyous and thrilling.

Suddenly Cody swept her off her feet and carried her over to the big bed. He didn't break their kiss until he laid her on it, and then he came down beside her. "Take off your nightgown," he said, his voice deep and low.

"But the lights—"

"I want to see you."

There was no doubting the desire in his silver-blue eyes. She'd never undressed in front of a man. Still, this was her husband, and he obviously wanted her. What was there to be afraid of?

The answer was obvious. She was afraid he'd see her flaws. She was afraid she wouldn't be perfect enough. But she couldn't let her shyness or lack of experience mar this moment. With her hands trembling, she reached for the hem of her nightgown and pulled it up and over her head.

Her nightgown slid to the floor as Cody reached for her to kiss her again. Then, just as their lips touched, a beeper on the dresser sounded.

He broke away with a low oath. "I have to get that."

"I know," she murmured, disappointed with the interruption, yet realizing this was Cody's life and hers, too. His responsibilities were important ones, and they'd have to make concessions for that.

Cody checked his pager and then picked up the phone and dialed. He listened for a short while, then said, "Call Dr. Singer. I'll need a consult on this one. I'll be there in ten minutes."

When he hung up the phone, he said, "I have to leave. I wish I didn't, but—"

"You're a doctor, Cody. I know patients come first."

He looked as if he wanted to say something, but he didn't. He just grabbed his jeans and an oxford shirt from his closet. "I don't know how late I'll be."

Picking up her gown, she slipped it on and sat on the edge of the bed.

After he stepped into his shoes, he came to her and lifted her chin, placing a light kiss on her lips. "I'll see you in the morning."

Then he pulled away and left.

Lauren watched him go, the longing inside her heart filling her whole being. What would happen when Cody came home? He sounded as if he expected her to be asleep. She knew he had early rounds in the morning. But if he wasn't gone long, maybe they could pick up where they'd left off. Maybe she'd truly become his wife.

Trying to occupy herself and keep her anticipation in check, she read for a while. Then, unable to really concentrate, she checked on Sara. The four-year-old was fast asleep, hugging her teddy bear. Back in the master bedroom Lauren turned off the light and heard each tick of the clock. She grew drowsy, but sleep wouldn't come. It was 2 a.m. when Cody came home.

He entered the bedroom without turning on a light and undressed in the dark. She thought about telling him she was awake, but it was late and he had to be tired. She didn't want him making love to her out of duty. She didn't want their first time to be rushed or less than it might be.

So she pretended to be asleep. When Cody got into bed, she was turned away from him. She heard him become still for a moment, as if maybe he was looking at her. But then he settled under the covers and turned the other way.

They'd connected earlier tonight. She'd felt it. She'd felt something from him that she'd never felt before. And she hoped she would feel it again.

Tomorrow was another day, and maybe it would be the real beginning of their marriage.

Sketching on a tablet on the patio table Monday afternoon, Lauren looked up every now and then to watch Sara on the swings. The March day was sunny, the temperature in the fifties. Taking advantage of the break from the winter, she'd taken Sara to the park on Saturday for some fresh air while Cody was at the hospital. Sara had enjoyed the outdoors so much that today Lauren had decided more time outside would be good for the four-year-old…and herself, too.

But Lauren was having a difficult time concentrating on the work she intended to show Craig Davis. She'd never had trouble concentrating on her work before. Yet, she'd never been married before, longing for a union with her husband that would unite their hearts and souls as well as their bodies.

She'd awakened this morning at five-thirty when Cody had gotten out of bed and started to dress. She'd said, "You didn't get much sleep."

But he'd continued dressing, responding, "I have to check on the patient I admitted last night. He had a severe asthma attack, and I want to make sure he's still stable. Go back to sleep. Sara won't be up for another couple of hours.''

Lauren had offered to make Cody breakfast, but he'd declined, saying he'd grab something at the hospital. He hadn't even kissed her, just told her to have a good day.

Maybe tonight they would have some time alone together. Maybe tonight...

Lauren struggled to focus her attention on the tablet in front of her and was startled to hear a yelp, then a cry from Sara. When Lauren looked up, Sara was on her hands and knees in front of the swing.

Seconds later Lauren was kneeling in front of her, asking, ''What happened, honey? Are you all right?''

Sara started to cry and between tears managed, ''My hands hurt. And my chin.''

Scooping the four-year-old onto her lap, Lauren hugged her tight. ''Did you fall off the swing?''

''I standed on the swing, like Jimmy, in the park. But I fell off.''

Lauren knew she should scold Sara but didn't have the heart. Holding her close, she rubbed her back soothingly, telling her everything would be okay. Finally Sara's tears subsided.

Sara's chin was red, and Lauren knew it would probably turn black and blue. ''We'll put some ice on your chin. It will make it feel better. Now let me look at your hands,'' she suggested. When she did, she saw they were scraped. ''Let's go into the bathroom and clean them up. We don't want them to get more sore later.''

''Will it hurt?''

Lauren knew honesty was the best policy, especially with children. "It might hurt a little when I wash them. But I bet your dad has something in the medicine cabinet that'll make them feel better."

Fifteen minutes later Sara was smiling again as she sat on Lauren's lap with bandages on both palms. Lauren held a small ice pack to Sara's chin while she read a story to her before nap time.

When Lauren tenderly kissed Sara's forehead, Sara wrapped her arms around Lauren's neck. "I like you here."

Lauren's eyes filled with tears as she realized how much she liked being here, and being a mother to Sara.

When Cody walked in the door at six o'clock that evening, he was tired and glad to be home. His patient was out of the woods, and Eli was on call this evening. Maybe tonight he and Lauren could finish what they had started last night.

It had been damn frustrating to walk away from her. But when he'd decided to practice family medicine, he'd known this would be his life. Gretchen had hated the interruptions. She'd hated the long hours. She'd hated attending cocktail parties, and then having him be paged and called away.

When he'd returned home last night, he'd wanted to awaken Lauren, hold her in his arms, kiss her and make her truly his wife. But they were walking a tenuous tightrope while combining their lives, learning each other's habits, each other's likes and dislikes. When they consummated their marriage, he didn't want her to be in a sleepy haze. He wanted to take time and care with her so that her first experience would pave the way for the rest of their marriage.

This morning he'd found it terribly difficult to leave with her looking so adorably sleep tousled. But he hadn't been able to trust himself to take just one kiss. He'd left, believing denial was better than giving in to desire he couldn't satisfy.

So when he stepped into the kitchen this evening and saw her looking delectably pretty in a turquoise-and-pink-patterned sweater and jeans, he convinced himself patience was of the utmost importance, and timing could be everything.

She smiled at him. "Hi. Dinner's almost ready. We're having spaghetti. Sara says it's one of her favorites."

His daughter had been sitting at the table, coloring, her back to him. But now she jumped off her chair and ran toward him. "Daddy, Daddy, see what I have!" And she held up both hands.

His daughter had obviously gotten injured somehow. He attempted to keep his worry and concern in check. But when he saw Sara's bruised chin, too, that was practically impossible. "What did you do?"

Sara told him about Jimmy standing on the swing at the park, and her trying it out on her own swing set.

All too intensely Cody remembered Gretchen's aptitude to slough off her responsibility for Sara to someone else, her desire to give her attention to community causes rather than their child.

"Where was Lauren while you were swinging?" he asked, attempting to remain calm and hear an adequate explanation for Lauren's lack of supervision of Sara.

"On the patio. She was coloring."

In other words she'd been working.

When he looked up at Lauren, her cheeks were flushed, and she looked guilty. "I was sketching."

"I see," he said somberly. Had he misjudged Lauren's abilities to mother? Would her work be more important than Sara? Would his daughter get pushed to the back burner while Lauren concentrated on what mattered most to her—her career?

He didn't want to bring it up now in front of Sara, but they'd have to talk about it later. He had to find out just how important Sara would be to her. Even with troubling thoughts clicking through his mind, when he looked at Lauren he wanted her. His physical need for her had been disconcerting all day. Now, in view of what had happened, it caused turmoil he'd never felt before.

After questioning Sara further, concerned that she'd bumped her head, he checked her over, making a game of shining his penlight into her eyes. She seemed okay.

But dinner was strained.

While Lauren cleaned up the dishes, he played hide-and-seek with his daughter, loving the sound of her giggles and squeals when he found her, pretending to be surprised when she found him. But all the while he wondered if he'd made a mistake marrying Lauren...wondered if she resented the time she'd be spending with Sara, rather than at the career she obviously loved. Sara would be going to kindergarten in the fall. That would give Lauren more freedom. But now how could he trust her with his daughter and depend on her to put Sara's needs first?

After Cody and Lauren put Sara to bed, he said to her, "Let's go downstairs and talk."

His desire for Gretchen had ebbed as he'd realized

she didn't *want* the deep intimacy he'd wanted and had diminished even more when he'd realized she disliked being a mother. But ever since last night the image of Lauren's naked body was burned in his mind. He was annoyed that he couldn't get it out of his head...especially when something more important was pressing on him—the welfare of his daughter.

Once he and Lauren were standing in the living room, he didn't beat around the bush. "Why weren't you watching Sara?"

"I was. But I was also working on a sketch. I only looked away for a few minutes—"

"In other words your attention was divided. And that's why my daughter got hurt. Lauren, I married you so your attention wouldn't be divided. Working in the sunroom with her nearby is one thing. But outside where she needs closer supervision... Never once under Kim's care did Sara get injured."

He could see the startled look in Lauren's eyes that told him she hadn't expected this reaction. Had she expected him to ignore his daughter's injuries? What if something worse than a bruise and scrapes happened to Sara...something that couldn't be fixed with bandages and a few soothing words? It was so difficult to protect his daughter when he wasn't with her. During his marriage to Gretchen, he'd constantly worried.

"I trusted you to keep Sara safe," he said, realizing he'd trusted Lauren in a way he'd never trusted Gretchen.

Lauren's expression filled with apology. "I'm sorry, Cody. I was distracted. But I *was* watching her."

"Apparently not well enough." A gut-deep disappointment made his voice rough, even angry.

Lauren looked hurt, and he couldn't handle gazing into her deep-brown eyes without wanting to take her into his arms. Yet he couldn't. "What's done is done," he said gruffly. "But I need your assurance that your work won't come before Sara."

"My work *doesn't* come before Sara," Lauren maintained.

"It did today, didn't it?"

They stared at each other, unable to close the gap between them.

When Lauren remained silent, he knew they were at an impasse. If she couldn't put Sara's welfare first...

Finally he said, "I have some work to do in my den. That's where I'll be if you need me."

She looked away from him, then squared her shoulders and met his gaze once more. "Will you be able to listen for Sara?"

"I'll turn on the monitor."

After only a moment's hesitation she crossed to the closet. "I'm going to drive over to the garden center. I need to pick up some catalogs from my office. I won't be long." Her voice was strained.

The distance between them was growing rather than decreasing. Didn't he want distance? Wasn't marriage safer that way?

"My purse is in the kitchen. I'll go out through the garage," she added in a tight voice as she put on her jacket.

And before he could blink, her ponytail swished over her shoulder, and she was gone.

When he heard her back her car out of the garage, he felt an emptiness that he'd never felt before.

Chapter Eight

Lauren's tears fell as she reached the parking lot at the garden center. They slid down her cheeks and she didn't bother to wipe them away. She'd had to leave Cody's house so she could get some perspective. Around him, she felt like a teenager again, needing to please him, wanting him to like her. It was silly. She was married to the man.

But she couldn't break through his barriers. He kept a wall around himself, and she wondered again if his love for Gretchen had been so deep that he could never open himself to anyone else.

Climbing out of her van, she used her key to unlock the padlock on the gate, and then she went to the closest greenhouse. Unlocking the door, she switched on the light. This greenhouse housed cyclamen in bright pink. Moving down the row, Lauren examined the leaves on the plants, the dampness of the soil in which they were potted, the color of the petals. As she drank in the essence of the flowers, she realized how they gave her balance, a sense of beauty, a feeling of being tied to the earth.

But even standing here where she usually felt peaceful, she felt pain and asked herself again if she'd done something wrong this afternoon. Should she have watched Sara more carefully? Should she have watched the four-year-old every minute? Is that what a mother was supposed to do? Yet thinking back on her own childhood and Rob's, she realized their parents had let them get their share of scrapes and bruises and bumps as they'd explored their world. Children needed supervision, but they also needed some space and the freedom to find out how they fit into the world around them.

Lauren walked up and down the rows, appreciated the flowers and thought about Sara and Cody until tears no longer fell and she felt calmer.

Suddenly from behind her she heard, "What are you doing here this late?"

Her brother acted as night watchman, making sure everything was secure, everything was in its place. If she told him nothing was wrong, he'd see right through her. He knew her too well.

"I needed some time to think."

After he walked down the aisle between the flower flats, he asked, "About your marriage?"

"I know you don't approve."

"It's not for me to approve or disapprove. But it sure happened awful quickly, and I have to wonder why."

"It's complicated, Rob."

He came closer. "Marriage is difficult enough without marrying for something other than the usual reasons...like being head-over-heels in love."

"I love Cody," she said, knowing it was true, feeling the love in every fiber of who she was.

He studied her for a very long time. "I think you've always loved Cody Granger. He has no idea how lucky he is."

She smiled at her brother's attempt to make her feel better. "You're biased."

"Possibly. But I'm right, too, aren't I?"

How could she tell her brother she had no idea what Cody's feelings were for her...if he felt any more than friendship? "I messed up today, Rob. I was taking care of Sara and not watching closely enough. She hurt herself. Not badly...but it never should have happened."

When he leaned against the table, he crossed his arms over his chest. "And Cody blames you?"

Tears came to her eyes again as she nodded.

After an assessing silence he said, "You're not going to solve anything by being here, you know. When two people argue, it's better to work it out than to run away from it."

Rob and Kim had been married for six years now, and they had a loving, solid relationship. Her brother knew what he was talking about. "Do you and Kim argue?"

"Sure, we do. But we made a pact before we were married. We never go to bed without talking about whatever causes us to argue. We might not be able to solve the problem right away, but we talk and we listen to each other, and sometimes it works itself out."

But they had a normal marriage. They went to bed every night and...

"Don't be too hard on yourself, Sis," he continued. "I can watch Matthew for twenty-four hours without blinking, and he'll still manage to get into some kind of scrape. That's the way kids are."

Somehow she had to balance what was her responsibility in this and what wasn't. But for now— She gave Rob a hug. "Thank you."

"Don't thank me yet. Wait until you get my bill."

She laughed and leaned back. "Do you want me to help you lock up again?"

He shook his head. "No need for that. I'm the best security guard I know. I'll make sure everything's tight, then I'll head home myself."

On the drive home Lauren realized she *wouldn't* get closer to Cody by running away from him. They needed to talk, and she had to tell him a few things that she'd realized as she'd searched her heart for answers.

It didn't take her long to drive back to Cody's house. Once inside, she hesitated only a few moments before hanging her jacket in the closet, then heading toward his den. The door was closed, and she knocked softly.

When Cody opened the door, he was still wearing his dress shirt and trousers, but his shirtsleeves were rolled up and his collar was open. The lines around his eyes were deep, and she remembered he'd had very little sleep the night before. In spite of that, she asked, "Can I come in?"

He stood aside to let her pass. She usually didn't bother him when he was in his den. There were two sets of oak bookshelves, an L-shaped desk with a computer monitor and printer to the side, and a black leather sofa that matched his swivel chair. The white walls were bare, and the window had a blind but no curtains.

She wished he would sit down, but he didn't, so she didn't, either. Rather, she plunged right in. "I'm sorry I didn't watch Sara more closely. I'll try to make sure that never happens again."

After studying her, he admitted, "Sara means everything to me, Lauren. I have to know I can trust her with you." His blue eyes were troubled.

"I know that. But sometimes children do the unexpected, and sometimes all the watching in the world can't protect them. I'm not trying to make excuses, but I can only do my best. Just as you can."

The silence in the room wrapped around them. And when Cody stepped closer, she didn't move away.

"Do you think you'll ever love Sara as your own daughter?" he asked.

She could sense that this was the underlying cause of his reaction to Sara's fall...the worry that she would never think of Sara as her own, love her as her own. Now his reaction made sense. Is this why he was keeping himself guarded?

Her love for him as well as Sara tightened her throat, but she managed, "I love Sara already, Cody. This afternoon before her nap, she put her arms around my neck and said she's glad I'm here. I—" Emotion filled Lauren, and she ducked her head.

Cody lifted her chin with his knuckle and saw the tears in her eyes. Pulling her into his arms, he held her, their heartbeats becoming one. After a few moments in his embrace, her heart started racing, and she thought his did, too. When she looked up at him, he said in a husky murmur, "I need you, Lauren."

And then he was kissing her, and she was wrapping her arms around his neck. Nothing in the world mattered but the two of them, holding each other, becoming closer.

The demand in Cody's kiss went far beyond anything he'd asked of her before. His tongue mated with hers...stroking...exploring...retreating, then coming back again. All the sensations rushing through her were stronger than any she'd ever felt. Her breasts tingled, and so did a place deep in her womb. She pressed into him and he groaned, backing her up to the sofa. Before she had a chance to breathe, let alone think, he was lifting her sweater over her head, then unsnapping her jeans. His undressing her was exciting...arousing. She wanted Cody in the way a wife wanted a husband. She wanted to know him in the true sense. She wanted the physical intimacy marriage should bring.

Cody drew in a breath, knowing his self-control was at the breaking point. He'd sat in his office for the past hour, unable to work, only able to think about Lauren. The frustration of wanting her day after day, yet keeping his need hidden, keeping his emotions in check, had cost him. Her declaration that she loved Sara, her fervent responses to his kisses told him she wanted this, too.

The fire of desire seemed to consume him as he finished undressing Lauren, rid himself of his own clothes quickly, then came down on top of her on the sofa. While he gave her another deep, long, excruciatingly sensual kiss, he stroked her breasts, and she opened her legs so that he fit between them. When he played with one nipple, she arched against him. Taking her cue, he put his lips to her breast, slid his tongue over and around, then teased her nipple until she moaned. While he continued to caress her breast, he lowered his hand and felt between her legs. She was wet and ready, and he couldn't wait to make her his wife.

The flames of passion pushed him on as he touched the center of her desire once, and then again. She writhed beneath him, murmuring his name.

"Are you ready for this, Lauren? Do you want me?"

"Yes, Cody. Yes!"

Her consent was all he needed. Propping on his elbows he positioned himself and then thrust inside.

She cried out. But when he started moving, she rocked with him, caught up in the moment, past the point of no return. He thrust deeper until she contracted around him and seemed to find her own pleasure as he took his. A few moments later his release came and he shuddered again and again.

Their bodies glistened with sweat as they lay still and silent.

He'd never intended their first time to be like this. He'd wanted to go slowly, make sure she knew pleasure each step of the way. But instead he'd let his desire take over, and now...

He felt shaken to his very core. He'd never become lost like that to a woman before. He'd never lost control. And the thing was, he didn't want to separate from her. He wanted to stay joined to her, and he wanted to do it again. He wanted to do it over and over and over, until the loneliness he'd felt all his life disappeared. He'd never even thought about such a thing with Gretchen. He'd always felt separate from her.

But with Lauren just now, for those few seconds, he'd felt as if they were one.

Looking down at her, he saw her eyes were closed. "Lauren?"

When she stared up at him, her brown eyes shimmered, and he didn't know what that meant. "Did I hurt you?"

"No...I...it was all just a surprise. So sudden. So fast."

She sounded close to tears, and he didn't know what to do about that. Damn it all. He might not only have hurt her, but he'd probably scared her, too. He'd acted like a caveman, and she would probably never forgive him for it.

After he separated from her and sat on the sofa, she dressed herself quickly as if she was embarrassed, as if she wanted to leave his den as fast as she could. "I'm going to go on up to bed," she said.

By the time he'd slipped on his trousers, she was at his office door. "I'll check in on Sara before I turn in. Good night, Cody."

She didn't even wait for his return good-night. He raked his hand through his hair and sank heavily into his desk chair.

How was he going to fix this?

Twice on Saturday afternoon Lauren tried to leave the garden center. Both times Rob insisted that she stay and help him with something...first with the display windows around the cashier's desk and then later with special orders that had come in during the past week. He usually did those himself, and she didn't understand why he needed her help.

Last night Cody had told her that he wanted to

spend some quality time with Sara this afternoon and asked Lauren if she'd mind if he took Sara to the movies and then for ice cream. Everything had been strained between them since the night they'd made love. Or rather, *she'd* made love. She hadn't been sure if she'd been more than a convenient release for Cody's sexual frustrations.

Everything that night had happened so fast. The heat, the passion, the conclusion. Since then Cody had kept his distance and hadn't touched her.

She didn't know what to do.

How did a woman find out if she was really important to a man? How did a wife tell her husband that she wanted him to touch her and kiss her and hold her? By just saying it?

Lauren sighed as she put the last of the invoices aside. She couldn't say it because she was afraid she'd been a monumental disappointment to him. She couldn't say it because she was afraid that he was comparing her to Gretchen.

His first wife was a ghost between them, and Lauren didn't know what to do about it.

It was five o'clock when Lauren left the garden center. As she parked in the garage, she saw that Cody's car was there. She thought about what she could make for supper. But when she went into the kitchen, Cody was standing at the counter waiting for her.

"I have something for you," he said.

He was wearing a red polo shirt and navy slacks and looked so sexy and virile that heat suffused her body. "Is Sara napping?" she asked.

"No. She's staying overnight with Kim." He handed Lauren a white envelope. "Open it."

Lauren didn't know what to expect. When she took out the note inside, the front of it said, "For Lauren."

Unfolding it, she read:

This is an invitation for you to attend the prom with me. If you accept, we'll have the best night of our lives.

                                                    Cody

Bemused, she looked up at him. "I don't understand."

Taking her hand, he said, "Come with me and you will."

When she stepped into what used to be the living room, she stepped into another world. There was a banner hanging across the room's archway that read "Lauren and Cody's Prom." She could smell flowers and saw four large bouquets, mixtures of roses and gladiolas, baby's breath and carnations in pink and yellow and white. The furniture had been moved against the wall, and a table sat to one side, covered by a white cloth. There were streamers hanging from the overhead light to the four corners of the room, and colorful helium balloons bobbed against the ceiling.

"Oh, Cody." Tears pricked her eyes, and she turned to him. "What did you do?"

He took both of her hands in his and tugged her closer to him. "I want tonight to be special, Lauren. I want to start over with you. To make up for any hurt I caused you. To make up for the other night. I never meant for things to get out of hand like that. You deserve better. You deserve to have me treat you gently, not like a Neanderthal claiming his woman.''

Trying to absorb what Cody was saying, Lauren shook her head. ''I didn't think that. I thought I'd disappointed you. I thought I did something wrong. You just shut off—''

''I felt guilty for coming on to you like that. I thought I'd rushed you...that you hadn't been ready.''

''I don't know if I was ready, but I wanted it, too. It was wonderful, Cody. Until you backed away.''

He swore and shook his head. ''Well, tonight I won't back away. Tonight we're going to do this right. I have something else for you.''

Going over to the sofa, he took a big white box from behind it and handed it to her.

She took it to the table and set it down, then opened the lid. ''Oh, Cody.''

It was a long dress, a beautiful shade of turquoise chiffon, that seemed to float over an underslip. The entire bodice was beaded.

''Kim picked it out. She said she was sure you'd like it.''

''It's beautiful,'' she murmured. ''I don't know what to say.''

''Say you'll wear it...say you'll dance with me tonight and let me show you how a new bridegroom should act with his bride.''

She couldn't keep her tears from overflowing and trickling down her cheeks. ''Yes, I'll spend tonight with you.''

Taking her into his arms then, he just held her for a very long moment. After he kissed her forehead, he leaned away. ''I have a few more things to take care of down here before I get dressed. My tux is in the den. Why don't you go upstairs and take a long bath, and I'll come up and knock on the door for you around six-thirty."

"Six-thirty it is," she said, wishing he'd kiss her.

But he just erotically rubbed his thumb across her lower lip. "It's a date." The gesture was a sensual reminder of what the night would bring.

Lauren took a bath, her excitement growing at the thought of the night ahead of her. After she brushed her hair until it shone, she put on the beautiful dress, adding a strand of pearls her parents had given her as a graduation present. When Cody knocked at the door, she was ready.

She opened it, and the look in his eyes made her feel beautiful and feminine and more confident in herself than she'd been in a long time. He looked exceedingly handsome in his tux, and she took his arm and let him escort her down the stairs. Soft music came from a CD player he'd set up in the corner, and candlelight flickered on the table set for two.

"I hope you like lobster," he said.

"I love lobster."

He pulled out a chair for her, and after she sat, he stooped close, his lips whispering against her cheek. "You look beautiful tonight."

Lauren couldn't believe Cody had gone to so much trouble. She couldn't believe all of this was real. It seemed like a romantic dream, but it was happening to her. And when she looked across the table at Cody, she knew her love for him was strong and deep and true—the way a love should be.

Did he feel the same way? She didn't know, but

tonight gave her hope...more hope than she'd ever had.

Cody disappeared into the kitchen for a few minutes and came back with two plates holding lobster tails, au gratin potatoes and green beans.

"How did you do this?" she asked.

"Kim gave me the name of a restaurant that does gourmet takeouts." He smiled at her, a crooked smile that was boyish, and smug, and altogether captivating.

They didn't talk much during the meal, just gazed into each other's eyes. In the midst of dinner Cody reached out and placed his hand over hers, rubbing his thumb over her fingers with a lingering sensuality that made her feel light-headed.

After they'd finished the main course, he smiled. "There's cheesecake and coffee for dessert. But we could dance first."

A slow, sentimental melody was playing. She nodded. "Let's dance."

When Cody took her into his arms, it was different than when they'd danced at their wedding. He held her closer to him, and everything about his expression told her that this was a prelude to intimacies he wanted to share with her.

With his lips very near to her cheek, he murmured, "I like holding you in my arms."

Gazing up at him, her heart beat so fast she could hardly speak. But she managed to say, "I like having you hold me."

At that he locked his hands at her waist and she twined her arms around his neck. Every movement was erotic. They were both aware of her breasts against his chest, her hips meeting his. His thighs were hard and powerful against her as they moved, and she felt as if she could sink into him...melt into him...become one with him.

When he bent his head to kiss her, they were still swaying to the music. But it became a cloud around them as she let him sweep her away with his lips and his tongue and his hands into a romantic dream. All she wanted was to make love with him again, to feel the freedom to touch him and to know that he wanted to touch her.

Then abruptly the sound of Cody's pager going off at his waist made him groan. After he pulled away from her, he said, "I'm not on call tonight, but I've got to answer it. It'll only take a minute." He kissed her again lightly, and it was a promise for more to come later.

She wandered back to the table as he strode across the room and picked up the cordless phone on the end table. His gaze held hers while he punched in the numbers almost automatically.

Then he looked away as someone came on the line, and his attention focused on the person speaking. "All right," he said. "I'll be there in ten minutes."

Lauren's heart sank at his words, and when he hung up the phone he looked as disappointed as she felt. "There's been a serious accident. Three cars were involved, and they need help at the hospital. Lauren, I'm sorry. I tried to make sure everything was perfect—"

"It was perfect, Cody. But I understand that you have to leave. It's okay." He was a doctor before all else, and she understood the commitment that went with that.

Reaching for her, he pulled her into his arms. "Maybe this won't take too long, and we can have cheesecake when I get home."

She lightly touched his jaw. "I'll be waiting for you."

Lauren's words stayed with Cody as he rushed into the emergency room just as the first ambulance arrived. Her words stayed with him as he consulted with Eli and then worked on one patient after another. He almost lost the young woman who had been driving the sports car that had caused the accident. But with the help of the crash cart he got her heart started again, and they wheeled her up to surgery.

There were no fatalities, but three of the patients were in serious condition. It was almost midnight before Cody felt he could leave.

What would Lauren be thinking? That he'd deserted her? That he'd disappointed her? That she'd never come first?

That had been one of Gretchen's major complaints.

Would Lauren react the same way? With distance and pouting and a look that made him feel guilty and frustrated at the same time?

Or would she simply be sleeping because it was late and she had no idea when he'd return?

At twelve-thirty, he pulled into his garage, then went into the house, his tuxedo and shirt over his arm. He'd changed into scrubs the first chance he'd gotten at the hospital.

There was a dim light glowing over the sink in the kitchen. He flipped it off and headed for the hall, where another light was still burning. When he went into the bedroom, he expected to see Lauren asleep. But she wasn't asleep. She was propped against the headboard with two pieces of cheesecake sitting on the bedside table.

She'd waited up. She didn't look disappointed but very happy to see him. His heart beat faster as desire for her again rushed through him. "I didn't think you'd wait up."

"I called the hospital about eleven-thirty and they said you should be home shortly. Are you too tired for dessert?"

He looked at the cheesecake, and then he looked at her. He'd never felt more invigorated. "I'm not too tired. Let me get a quick shower. I'll be back in five minutes."

And he was, with his hair still damp.

Lauren blushed slightly when she saw he was naked. As he gazed at her, he became more aroused, and her cheeks became even rosier.

Walking over to her side of the bed, he looked down at her. "I think cheesecake tastes better when you don't have any clothes on."

"Cody…"

He sat beside her hip. "What can I do to make you less embarrassed? To help you be less shy with me?"

Indignantly she sat up straight. "I'm *not* shy."

He arched his brows.

"Well, I'm *not*. Not when I know—" She stopped.

"Know what?" he asked gently.

"Not when I know you want me as much as I want you."

Her admission had come out in a rush, and nothing she said could have pleased him more. His already-heated blood raced faster, and he held her chin in his palm. "I want you, Lauren. There's no doubt about that. And this time we're going to do this right...slow and sweet until we're both begging for it."

As he pulled back the sheet, she lifted her gown up and off. They gazed at each other as they lay face-to-face.

Cody's desire became a necessary need, one he'd never felt this deeply before. Although his body longed to race toward completion, he would keep his word and make this as good for Lauren as he possibly could. Sliding his hand into her hair, he gave and took a full, long kiss. Then very slowly, he pulled away and let his lips travel down her neck to the vee between her breasts. There he played and taunted and aroused with his lips and tongue...until she laced her fingers in his hair. Lauren's responses urged him on, and he felt powerful and strong in a way he'd never felt before.

Yet when she touched him, he knew *he* wasn't the one with the power. *She* was. And she didn't even seem to know it.

The feel of her fingers in his chest hair made him groan, and she asked, "Am I doing something wrong?"

Chuckling, he brought her hand to his lips and kissed her palm. "You're doing everything right. Touch me anywhere you want. Kiss me anywhere you want. Explore me as I want to explore you, Lauren. That's what being married is all about."

Although Lauren was shy, he felt a freedom with

her he hadn't felt in his entire life. They were mutually giving and taking. There were no wild undirected hormones; nor was there a sense of duty. There was real sharing—of touches, of kisses, of responses—that told the other it was so good.

Restraining himself took its toll on Cody. Beads of sweat formed on his brow. But he was determined to make this night one Lauren would never forget.

He was placing soft, nipping kisses around her navel when she clutched his shoulders. "I want you inside me, Cody. Please. Now."

The boldness in Lauren's request almost pushed him over the edge. She was free with him, like a butterfly who'd finally broken out of its cocoon.

When he raised himself on his elbows, he gazed into her eyes and saw the same longing he felt...the same need to reach the stars together. He entered her with an excruciating slowness that took his breath away. Then he withdrew, and she arched up toward him as if she couldn't bear to be separated from him.

As he came to her again, she pleaded, "Don't tease me."

"I'm not. I'm prolonging it for us both."

"I want you now, Cody. We can always do it again."

He laughed, so deep and free, he hardly recognized the joyful sound as his own. Then he was inside her, moving to her rhythm as well as his...thrusting deeper and deeper until he was completely lost in her.

"Cody, I never imagined this would be so...so—"

She stopped, and he drove harder until she gripped his shoulders and called his name.

His climax hit at the same moment, and he shuddered...never, *ever* experiencing anything so mind shattering.

So world shattering.

Chapter Nine

It was a Wednesday afternoon, and Lauren was preparing dinner, thinking about the six weeks since the prom night Cody had planned for her...thinking about her missed period. Tomorrow morning when she and Sara ran errands, she was going to pick up a pregnancy test.

Everything had been going so smoothly. She'd had fun turning their house into a real home—decorating, finding curtains and a spread for Sara's room, adding color to the first floor. This past week she'd finished landscaping the pond in the backyard. Her life seemed completely full, especially since she'd gotten the contract on the office complex in Denver. The day she'd received the call, Cody had brought home a bottle of champagne, and they'd toasted her success, making love long into the night.

Everything seemed so perfect...they were growing closer. In bed, at least, it seemed that all of Cody's barriers were down.

But she could tell he was still holding back. If she was pregnant...

Suddenly she was startled by two strong arms wrapping around her. But as she caught the scent of spicy cologne and recognized her husband's embrace, she relaxed. "I didn't hear the garage door go up."

Brushing her hair aside with his chin, he kissed her neck. "You were deep in thought. Designing a garden in your mind?"

Forgetting the salad fixings in the sink, she turned into his arms and faced him. "No. Thinking about us."

"So am I. I finished up early and don't have to be at the hospital for about an hour." His blue eyes gleamed with desire. "Is Sara napping?"

"Yep. I thought I'd get a head start on supper. Want to help?" she teased, knowing why he'd come home, why she was already trembling.

He began unfastening the top button of her blouse. "I can think of something a lot more exciting to do." He kissed her neck again, then trailed soft, wet kisses down to her breasts.

The pleasure he gave her was always a surprise and a gift. As he unbuttoned her blouse and pulled it from her jeans, his mouth teased and taunted the outline of her breasts, and she moaned softly. "Cody, we should go upstairs," she breathed.

Unsnapping her bra, he shook his head. "I think the kitchen floor is looking awfully good right now. We *could* try to make it to my den—"

The telephone rang. By the second ring, he raised his head. Snatching the receiver off its base, he gave her a wry smile. They had had more than one untimely interruption over the past weeks, but they'd both become accustomed to it. Actually, there was even more excitement and pleasure when they finally could fulfill what they'd begun.

But as Cody answered the phone, his expression became serious and then... "Yes, we'll be there, Frank. What time?"

After a few more polite comments, Cody hung up the phone. When he looked at her, there was a change in him.

Lauren refastened her bra. "What is it?"

"That was the chairman of the board of the hospital in Colorado Springs. He'd like me to be there Sunday afternoon to present me with an award for Gretchen...for the contributions she made to the fund-raising of the new hospital wing."

"Are you on call this weekend?"

"Eli and I will work it out."

Feeling as if she were plunging into unchartered territory, she asked, "Do you want me to come along?"

He only hesitated a moment, but the hesitation was there. "Yes, I would."

She wanted to ask *why*. She wanted to ask how he still felt about Gretchen. But she was afraid of his answer...afraid she'd ruin the happiness of the past few weeks.

He glanced at his watch. "I should get to the hospital."

The mood had definitely been broken, and although they would have had time for a quick bout of lovemaking, she could tell it wouldn't be a good idea. Cody had put up a wall between them again.

What would it take to tear it down?

* * *

As Lauren ladled punch into a cup for Sara, she glanced around the large community room at the hospital in Colorado Springs. Sara was seated next to Dolores, munching on a cookie, swinging her legs and talking a mile a minute. Dolores looked on fondly, and Lauren knew no matter what Cody thought of his former mother-in-law, she did care about her granddaughter. When Lauren looked for Cody, she found him standing in one corner of the room, talking to a bearded gentleman in a black suit.

Since the phone call inviting Cody to receive this award for Gretchen, he'd become removed again. Quieter. More distracted. Lauren believed he was still struggling with his grief for his wife.

Cody's remoteness worried her. She'd used the pregnancy test, and it had been negative. So she hadn't said anything to him. But since she'd missed her period, she wanted to make sure. She had an appointment with Eli tomorrow morning while Cody was at the hospital making rounds. If she *was* pregnant, she wasn't sure how he'd react to the news. *She'd* be overjoyed, because a baby would be an incontrovertible bond between them.

After Lauren carried Sara's drink to her and sat down beside her, Cody came over and took a seat next to Lauren. His shoulder brushed hers as he handed her the program pamphlet. "I hope this won't be too long for Sara."

Lauren looked over at her stepdaughter who was cheerfully munching on another cookie. "She'll be fine. If she gets restless, I can always take her for a walk."

"She's becoming attached to you," Cody said,

with something that looked almost like pain in his eyes.

Was he thinking about everything that Gretchen wasn't going to be able to share with her daughter? Did he feel torn by the affection Sara was beginning to show for Lauren? Lauren wished he would talk to her about it. She wished he'd talk to her about everything that was on his mind.

The chairman, Mr. Hollis, came to the microphone and gave a short, welcoming speech. Then he explained what the new emergency wing meant to the hospital and the lives it would save. A few minutes later the director of emergency services gave a brief explanation of the innovations and technological advances that would serve the community. Afterward the chairman again stepped in front of the podium.

Looking out over the audience, his eyes found Cody and then Dolores. He smiled at them and said, "I have a special plaque to give to the family of someone who is missed here. Gretchen Granger gave her time and her energy to many causes in the community. The new emergency room wing was a priority to her. Because of her effort we met our financial goal and were able to start in record time. Now that the emergency room wing is complete, unfortunately Gretchen is not with us to see it. We sorely miss her, and we certainly have not forgotten her. In order to prove that, I'd like to ask her husband, Dr. Cody Granger, to come up here, please."

Cody stood and walked toward the front of the room to the podium.

Mr. Hollis held out a plaque to him. "This is to commemorate Gretchen's contributions to this hospital and this community. We'd like you to take this plaque home, so that you have a tangible acknowledgment of our appreciation of her gift. In addition we will be hanging a memorial plaque in the lobby of the emergency wing."

Cody's words and thanks were brief, but that was understandable. This recognition of Gretchen's contributions had to be difficult, as well as satisfying. When he returned to his seat he sat very still, and Lauren had never felt more distance between them. The minutes seemed to slowly tick by until Mr. Hollis completed the rest of the program, finally inviting everyone to tour the new wing.

Well-wishers and old acquaintances spoke to Cody and Dolores, too, most of them expressing their sorrow at losing Gretchen. Cody's face became more and more strained.

When everyone finally dispersed, Dolores asked Cody, "May I see the plaque?"

Tears filled her eyes as he held it while she studied the inscription. "Are you going to hang this in Sara's room?" she asked.

"I'll either do that or put it in the drawer where I have other things of Gretchen's." His voice was even, but there was a world of turmoil in his eyes.

"It should be someplace where she can see it, so she knows what good work her mother did," Dolores maintained. "It shouldn't lie in some drawer... forgotten."

"Sara can go into the guest bedroom and look through that drawer anytime she wants."

Sara hopped off her chair and looked up at Cody. "Can we go home now?"

Stooping down, he lifted his daughter into his arms

and held her as if she were the most precious child on earth. "Yes, we can."

"Aren't you going to tour the emergency wing with everyone else?" Dolores asked.

"We toured it when we arrived. Sara's missed her nap, and I think we'd better be going."

Dolores's frown was clearly disapproving. "Racing off again. You *could* come over to the house."

Cody said patiently, "Another time."

After Dolores studied him, she looked defeated when she said, "All right."

Cody was silent on the drive back to Birch Creek, and Lauren didn't know whether to probe or leave well enough alone. Finally she decided to tackle the subject of Gretchen. "I imagine accepting that award for Gretchen was very hard for you today."

He kept his gaze on the road. "I was proud of the work she did in the community."

"What else was she involved in?" Lauren asked softly, treading lightly.

Cody glanced at her. "You name the charity, Gretchen raised money for it—cancer, diabetes, muscular dystrophy."

"You two must have made a good team."

When Cody didn't respond, Lauren let the subject drop. It was obvious he didn't want to talk about his marriage, and maybe it was better if she didn't remind him how good he and Gretchen were together.

It was early evening when they arrived home. After fixing a light supper, they put Sara to bed. Then Cody said, "I'm going to work in my den."

Should she let him shut her out? Should she give him the space he obviously wanted? She had no choice. If she pried and questioned, he might put even more distance between them.

And if she was pregnant?

The thought scared her, but also gave her hope.

In his den Cody flipped on his computer, but then swiveled away from it to look out the window. Accepting that award in Gretchen's honor had been *more* than difficult. He'd felt like a damn hypocrite. How many times had they argued about her charity work? How many times had he prayed she would stay home and take care of their daughter, rather than run to meetings and organize auctions? By the time Gretchen died, their marriage had been in so much trouble he hadn't known how to dig out from it. The love he'd once felt for her had dissipated into worry for his daughter and frustration that he couldn't make things right.

He was torn when it came to telling Sara about her mother. He could tell her Gretchen had been beautiful. He could tell her she'd done good works in the community. But he couldn't tell Sara how much her mother had loved her. He couldn't tell Sara that her mother had treasured her and cherished her as a child should be cherished. His chest tightened when he thought of the times he'd come home and found Sara with a baby-sitter or over at Dolores's.

Whenever Gretchen took care of Sara, there was no warmth. It was duty. She kept saying that once Sara got older, maybe she could relate to her better. He remembered again how he'd tried to convince Gretchen to go for counseling and how he'd finally ordered her to go. But she'd evaded him, made an appointment and then canceled it…made another and found an excuse not to go again.

Why hadn't he seen what kind of woman Gretchen was before Sara was born? If he hadn't met her when he was so young, maybe her charm and beauty and sexuality wouldn't have wound themselves about him until he couldn't see straight, where she was concerned.

But now he was married to Lauren. And in the past six weeks he'd felt more whole than he could ever remember. He felt as if he had a friend. And when they had sex—

It unsettled him, and he felt too vulnerable. He'd guarded against vulnerability all his life.

Finally turning back to his desk, he went online and accessed a medical library he often used. But he couldn't forget the way Lauren had looked as she'd read Sara a story tonight before bedtime. He couldn't forget about how he became aroused whenever she smiled at him or inadvertently touched him. He couldn't forget the way he looked forward to coming home to her.

With an act of sheer will, he concentrated on what was on the screen before him, determined to make this marriage different from the first…determined to keep his boundaries set.

On Tuesday afternoon when the phone rang, Lauren heard Eli's voice and held her breath.

"Lauren, I'm sorry," Eli said. "You're not pregnant."

Her heart fell. "But I missed my period…."

"That's why I did the blood test, to make absolutely sure. You've had so many changes in your life recently. Marriage. Being a mother to Sara. It's not unusual for stress to throw off a woman's cycle.''

Tears filled her eyes. "But I was so hoping..." Her voice caught, and she stopped.

"I know you were. But you and Cody have been married less than two months. Give it a little time."

Since Sunday Cody had seemed so removed from her. She was hoping if she was pregnant, if she could give him that news, they could find the closeness they'd felt the last few weeks. She'd thought if they had the bond of a pregnancy, Cody would really let her in.

"Thanks for calling, Eli."

"You know, don't you, that when you and Cody do have children, I'm going to act like a doting grandparent," Eli assured her.

She tried to smile. "I would imagine there's nothing Cody would like more."

After Lauren said goodbye to Eli, she felt like crying. But crying wouldn't do any good. Instead she would make a special supper and the chocolate cake Cody liked so much. Then maybe after they put Sara to bed, he'd have a second piece and they could sit and really talk....

But at five o'clock, when she was mixing icing with Sara looking on, Cody called to tell her he'd be late. He'd gotten backed up with patients this afternoon, and he still had rounds to make at the hospital. It might be nine o'clock when he got home.

Disappointed but not daunted, Lauren told him she'd make a plate for him and ended simply with, "I'll be here waiting for you."

She took Sara to the park after supper until almost dusk, then they walked home hand in hand. Lauren loved the feel of Sara's little fingers engulfed in hers. She loved being a mother. Maybe soon she would get pregnant. Tonight she'd ask Cody if he wanted a child as much as she did.

While Sara was brushing her teeth, Lauren went downstairs to fetch clean laundry she'd forgotten in the dryer. After she returned upstairs and set the wash basket in the master bedroom, she couldn't find Sara in the bathroom or in her room. Lauren panicked and called Sara's name.

"Here I am," the four-year-old called, her voice sounding muffled.

Hurrying toward the sound of Sara's voice, Lauren found her in the guest bedroom. She was sitting on the floor in front of a chest of drawers, the bottom drawer pulled out.

"Daddy put Mommy's 'ward here," Sara explained, peering into the drawer as if it were a treasure trove.

Sara and the contents of the drawer drew Lauren inside the guest bedroom. What mementos had Cody kept? What memories of Gretchen did he want to keep alive? What keepsakes were important enough for Sara to have access to?

As Lauren went into the room, she saw everything spread out around Sara. There were photographs, a jewelry case and knickknacks.

Not knowing exactly how to handle the situation, Lauren sat on the floor next to her. "What are you doing?"

"Lookin'. Daddy lets me look when I want to."

Picking up a blue ribbon from a riding competition, Lauren held it in front of Sara. "Do you know what this is?"

Sara shook her head.

Apparently Cody hadn't explained the meaning behind everything in the drawer. Lauren told Sara about riding horses and showing them to see who was the best rider. Her mommy had won a ribbon for being one of the best.

Next Lauren picked up a photograph of Gretchen in her cheerleading uniform with her pom-poms. "I knew your mommy," Lauren told Sara.

"You did?" Her eyes, so much like her father's, were wide with curiosity.

"Mmm-hmm. We went to the same high school together, with your daddy. Your mom was a great cheerleader." Seeing bits of plastic sticking up out of the drawer, Lauren extricated one of the pom-poms. "Your mommy used this."

"What's a cheerleader?" Sara asked.

"Someone who gets the crowd all excited to help the football team win. Maybe in the fall we can go to a football game."

As Lauren looked through the drawer with Sara, she saw the evidence of everything Gretchen had accomplished. How beautiful she was. How perfect she was. Did Cody still think about her all the time? When he went to bed at night? When he held Lauren in his arms? Could he help but compare?

Would Lauren feel like a substitute for the rest of their marriage?

Telling herself she couldn't give in to jealousy, she went through the items one by one with Sara, hoping that someday Sara would think of her as her mother.

When Lauren glanced at her watch, she saw that it was well past Sara's bedtime. "Come on, honey. Let's get you to bed. I'll put this away later."

After Lauren read Sara a story, she gave her a good-night kiss.

"When's Daddy coming home?"

Lauren closed the book and put it on the bedside table. "I don't know, but I'm sure he'll stop in and give you a good-night hug, even if you're not awake."

Sara wrapped her arms around Lauren's neck. "Give you another hug."

Tears of happiness and warmth and fulfillment came quickly to Lauren's eyes. She loved this little girl so much already.

After she left Sara's room, knowing she should just put all the keepsakes away, Lauren couldn't help but linger over each one again. She was on her knees at the bottom drawer, putting the pom-pom back in, when she heard footsteps in the hall.

As Cody passed the room, he saw her and stopped still. When he came in, he asked, "What are you doing?"

He looked troubled about finding her here, so she explained quickly. "I went downstairs for fresh laundry, and when I came back up, Sara had pulled everything out of the drawer. She didn't know what some of the things were, like the blue ribbon and the pom-poms, so we talked about each one for a little while."

Cody's expression was stern and grim. "And just what did you tell her?"

"I told her I knew her mommy, and that she was a great cheerleader, and very, very beautiful. You don't talk to Sara much about her mother, so I thought I—"

"I talk to her when she asks me about her."

He had told her that once before. But this time Lauren wasn't going to let it drop. It was time they talked about Gretchen. "Have you saved other re-membrances…besides the things in this drawer?"

He'd apparently shed his suit coat downstairs, and now he tugged down his tie. "I have Gretchen's valuable jewelry in a safe-deposit box."

Shoring up more courage than she ever knew she had, she asked, "Is your wedding ring there, too?"

The silence in the room was deafening as his blue gaze probed hers. "What do you want to know, Lauren?"

Their marriage couldn't succeed without complete honesty. It also couldn't succeed if there was no hope that he'd love her. She had to find out exactly what his feelings were. "I need to know if you're still in love with Gretchen."

Several heartbeats pounded in her chest until he said roughly, "Love? I'm not sure I even know what that is."

His statement took her aback. "The way you're grieving for Gretchen, you must have felt it deeply—"

The turmoil she'd only glimpsed in him before became etched on his face when he cut in, "I loved Gretchen, all right. I loved her until I couldn't see straight. Until I couldn't see anything else. She was my reason for succeeding. She was my reason for putting in the long hours in college and in med school. I lived for once-a-month visits with her, and I thought she lived for them, too. Now I don't know."

"I don't understand." Lauren's heart raced faster

as she saw the tension in Cody…in his stance as well as his fists clenched at his sides.

"It turns out that Gretchen wanted the prestige of being a doctor's wife and the income that went with it," he said. "But she hated my long hours and emergency calls. She wanted to be a wife, but she didn't want to be a mother."

That revelation was hard for Lauren to absorb. "She didn't want to have a baby?"

Cody looked as if he'd been turned to stone. He said almost coldly, "She hated the thought of her pregnancy because it would ruin her figure. And she left Sara in Dolores's care more than she took care of her herself."

Then he gazed squarely into Lauren's eyes. "I poured my heart and soul into that marriage, and I still couldn't make it succeed. I couldn't make her want to spend time with her daughter. I couldn't prove that my love for her was better and more important than the lifestyle she thought she deserved."

Shocked by his words, Lauren rose to her feet, finally realizing what he was saying. "You weren't happy with Gretchen?"

His mouth twisted wryly. "Happy? Knowing our marriage disintegrated a little more every day? Knowing that no matter what I did, it wasn't enough? No, I wasn't happy. And when Gretchen died, I swore I'd never give that much of myself to anyone again, except for Sara."

Never give that much of himself to anyone except Sara.

The vehement declaration seemed to echo inside of Lauren. The hurt she felt went so deep, she could hardly breathe. She'd held on to the hope that he would one day love her. But if he wouldn't *let* himself love, that could never happen.

All she could say was, "You said marriage vows meant something to you."

"They do. That's why I didn't divorce Gretchen. I thought we could work it out. I thought with time, with counseling, she'd learn to mother Sara."

It was obvious he was still living his first marriage, the pain from it...the disappointment. If only she'd known. "What about *our* marriage vows?" she asked, praying he would give her a sign that they could overcome whatever had happened in the past.

He raked his hand through his hair. "I meant the vows, Lauren. I promised to be faithful, and I will be. I promised to take care of you, and I'll do that."

She didn't want to be taken care of. She wanted to be *loved*. "I know we married because of Sara, but marriage is all about pouring your heart and soul into it. When I made my vows to you, I made them with faith and hope and everything I was. No limits. Cody, a successful marriage can't have limits! If both people don't give everything they have, everything they are—"

With a shake of his head, he cut her off again. "That's an illusion, Lauren. Happily-ever-after is something you only read about in books."

"That's not true! My mom and dad have that kind of marriage, and so do Rob and Kim. Just because you've never experienced it doesn't mean it doesn't exist."

The silence in the room hung between them, as tangible as her words.

"Do you want out?" he asked grimly.

No, she didn't want out. She loved him. But if he

couldn't love her... "What I want I don't think you can give me."

Hoping with all of her heart he would tell her that she was wrong, she prayed he would say that he needed her...that in time his feelings would grow...that maybe marriage could come to mean something very special to him again.

But Cody said nothing.

Lauren suspected that he'd guarded himself for so long he didn't know how to shrug off the protection. He didn't know how to want more than he had. He didn't know how to open his heart to her.

It seemed that she'd loved Cody for as far back as she could remember. But it was about time *she* had some pride, too. She couldn't let him know how much she loved him. She couldn't let him see how much he'd hurt her. "We were wrong to marry because of Sara. A child can't be the basis of a marriage...at least not the kind of marriage I want."

"Then you *do* want out," he concluded gruffly.

"I want the devotion I see every time my mom and dad look at each other. I want a bond that nothing can destroy."

"You want the impossible."

She shook her head sadly. "If you think it's impossible, then I'd better leave before Sara gets any more attached to me."

As she said the words, her heart still hoped he would stop her...that he'd realize if they both believed, they could live happily ever after.

But his expression didn't change, and the nerve in his jaw worked. Finally he stated, "You're right. It would be best for Sara if you left now."

He was telling her he couldn't believe in

love…that their marriage had never been real…that the past weeks had meant nothing.

She couldn't make him want something he didn't want. She couldn't give him the faith to believe in them as a couple. Moving toward the door, she felt so cold…so alone. "I'll pack a suitcase and leave tonight. You can drop the rest of my things off at my parents' house. That's where I'll be until I find an apartment again. I'll say a last goodbye to Sara before I go."

Cody didn't react. He didn't stop her. He let her go into the hall without a word.

With tears filling her eyes, Lauren went to the master bedroom, pulled her suitcase from the closet and packed quickly. Then she set her suitcase outside of Sara's door as she went in to the little girl she was beginning to think of as her daughter.

Sara's black curls wisped around her face as she slept on her side.

Lauren's heart felt as if it were breaking as she leaned down, kissed Sara's cheek and told her goodbye.

While Lauren carried her suitcase down the steps and out to her car, tears kept falling. As she backed out of Cody's driveway, her sobs broke loose. Her heart *was* breaking, and there was no way she'd ever put it back together again.

A half hour after Lauren left, Cody felt absolutely numb. He went into his daughter's room and stared at Sara for a very long time. Then he looked around her room. There were curtains at the windows now, white eyelet with pink ribbon running through the edges. Lauren had framed a few of Sara's drawings, and they hung on the wall, too. An angel mobile dangled from one corner, and the spread that lay across Sara's bed was appliqued with kittens and puppies.

All of it was Lauren's doing.

As Cody went downstairs, he saw the same evidence of Lauren's presence. Knickknacks filled the hutch now, and a silk-floral centerpiece decorated the table. In the living room, she'd hung a colorful tapestry on the wall above the sofa and placed throw pillows in the corners. There was a scatter rug on the floor in front of the archway and dried flowers in a vase on the bookshelves.

Lauren had added warmth everywhere she'd touched.

And now she was gone.

Feeling as if he were sleepwalking, Cody stopped in the kitchen and saw the chocolate cake on the counter. When he went outside, he was drawn to the pond and garden that Lauren had designed. He sat on a chair there for a long, long time.

When he finally went up to bed, he felt as if his world had stopped and it would never start again.

His sleepless night allowed him hours of self-examination and reflection. He saw emotions clearly for the first time in two years, and he counted every mistake he'd made.

The morning sun brought questions for him from Sara. Where was Lauren? When would she be back?

He found himself afraid to give his daughter answers because then they'd be real. So he told her Lauren had to go away for a while.

Fortunately, he didn't have office hours this morning. He called his receptionist to see if she could juggle afternoon appointments, rescheduling any that weren't urgent. Then he phoned Dolores.

When she answered, he said, "I owe you an apology."

There was silence for a few moments.

Then he went on, giving her some of the answers he'd found in the dead of night. "I was angry at Gretchen. Still am, I guess. For not being the kind of mother I wanted her to be to Sara. Since she died, I've been taking that anger out on you."

After a very long pause, Dolores finally admitted, "I know Gretchen wasn't the mother she should have been to Sara. I tried to talk to her about it many times. But she wouldn't listen. She'd just tell me she didn't want to be stuck at home all the time. But it went deeper than that, and I guess I blamed myself. That's why I wanted to help you so much with Sara—" she sighed "—but you didn't want my help. You didn't want Sara to be anywhere near me."

Throughout the night Cody had examined everything he'd done, everything he'd said and everything he'd felt since Gretchen had died. "I was wrong. You love Sara, and she needs you in her life."

"Are you going to let her come spend some time with me?" There was a catch in Dolores's voice.

"Actually I have a lot of thinking to do, and it might be better if Sara stayed with you for a few days. But I understand that this is very short notice—"

"Nonsense. What else do I have to do? Play tennis? Have lunch with my bridge club? Sara's much more important to me than that, Cody."

"I know she is." Deep down he'd always known that.

"When can you bring her?"

"How about this morning?"

"That sounds wonderful. I can't tell you how much this means to me. Your phone call... everything."

Cody realized how his anger had kept a barrier between himself and Dolores and how his honesty had torn it down. Maybe they could be friends now.

Most of the way to Colorado Springs, Cody sang songs with Sara to keep her from getting restless. But his heart wasn't in it.

He felt as if he'd lost his heart.

Sara had loved the idea of staying with her grandmother for a while, and when Cody left her there, he knew he was doing the right thing. He told Dolores to page him if she needed anything, and he'd call this evening just to make sure Sara still wanted to stay overnight.

Since his receptionist had rescheduled three-quarters of his appointments, by three o'clock Cody was finished seeing his patients. He still had to make rounds at the hospital, but before he did that...

He needed to take out his motorcycle.

At home he heard the silence of the empty house again. He changed into jeans and a T-shirt and wheeled his bike out of the garage. Then he mounted it, revved it and took it from Birch Creek onto the interstate so he could feel the wind around his body and the freedom of the speed.

He rode and rode and rode. But today it wasn't the calming experience it usually was. Eventually returning to his hometown, he veered toward the creek and the path along it, remembering the first night he'd taken Lauren riding on his bike. He knew he was going faster than he should, but he could still almost feel her arms around him. Smell her sweet scent. Hear her soft voice—

Suddenly there was something streaking in front of him on the path. A squirrel...a small dog...a fox? He didn't know what it was. He just knew he didn't want to hit it, and he swerved as the speed took him forward. The motorcycle went into a slide. When the dust settled, the bike was lying on top of his leg.

For a few moments Cody didn't move.

Pushing the weight of the bike from him and removing his helmet, he saw the nasty scrape on his forearm and elbow. There was a gash on his leg where his jeans had torn. His face felt hot, and when he put his hand to his jaw, there was blood on his fingers. And it hurt to breathe. He must have bruised his ribs.

So much for the freedom of speed.

Struggling to his feet, he went to lift the bike, the pain in his ribs making him bend over and suck in a breath. Then he tried again. But when he managed to get himself upright on the bike, it wouldn't start.

Why hadn't he brought his cell phone?

Because his mind had still been trying to wrap itself around the fact that Lauren had left.

Leaving the bike and helmet on the ground and trying to ignore the pain in his leg, he started walking.

Chapter Ten

Eli had tended to Cody's leg and arm and was now examining his ribs.

Cody sucked in a breath as Eli probed.

"They're going to hurt for a while," his old mentor said. "And you should really stay off that leg. I think I might have a cane in the supply room. Why didn't you stop at the first pay phone you came to instead of walking all the way here?"

"I knew you had patients."

"You could have called Lauren."

Cody was beginning to ache all over but didn't think it had as much to do with his accident as it did with something much more elemental. "She's... working today," he hedged.

Eli finished with his exam and took antiseptic in hand to apply it to Cody's face. To distract his patient, Eli kept talking. "Are you as disappointed as she is that she's not pregnant?"

Pregnant? "I didn't know she *might* be." The words spurted out before Cody could catch them.

"Uh-oh. Did I let the cat out of the bag? I'd better let you talk to her about it. That girl thinks the sun rises and sets with you. She gave me the impression that having your baby would be the most wonderful thing that could ever happen to her."

Cody looked Eli straight in the eye. "I don't think she sees it that way anymore."

After a long pause Eli asked, "Do you want to tell me what happened?"

Cody was still trying to sort it all out. "I thought this marriage would be reasonable...practical. Lauren and I look at the world the same way. She's so different from Gretchen...so loving and giving."

If Eli was surprised he hid it well and merely asked reasonably, "So what's the problem?"

The problems circled in Cody's head—his tunnel vision when he'd married Gretchen, his frustration that he couldn't fix whatever was wrong with his marriage to her, his anger with Dolores. But most of all his attitude toward marriage that had kept him frozen in the past instead of living in the present with Lauren. "I wanted to stay safe. I didn't want to feel. I didn't want to fail again. But Lauren left last night, and I feel as if I've dived into a black hole with no bottom."

"Mmm," Eli grunted. "Apparently you *are* feeling. You're feeling so much you don't know how to act or what to do about it."

The confusion inside Cody tumbled over the pain. "Something like that. I don't know, Eli. I gave Gretchen everything I could, and she threw it back in my face. Lauren gave me so much—"

Eli concluded, "And you threw it back in hers?"

The extent of what Cody had done weighed on him. "Yes, I did."

Silence in the room emphasized the seriousness of Cody's words.

"I'll go look for that cane," Eli said. "Then I'll take you home. You need to get off your feet and rest. I can cover your rounds tonight."

While Cody waited for Eli, he began to realize the depth of his feelings for Lauren. Just because he'd denied having them for weeks didn't mean they weren't there. Besides that, he'd better be honest with himself and call a spade a spade.

He didn't just have feelings for Lauren...he loved her.

He didn't know when or how it had happened. Had this true, deep feeling begun so many years ago when he'd liked being in her company? Or had it begun the first time he'd seen her after his return to Birch Creek? It had certainly taken root when she'd begun caring so tenderly for his daughter.

He'd been denying so many things—his anger at Gretchen, his anger at himself for failing at a marriage he couldn't save. He could see now, so clearly, that he'd been drawn to Lauren because of her warmth, her unselfishness, her giving heart. Somehow after all these years she'd forgiven him for hurting her, and now he'd hurt her again.

He'd hurt her by not feeling their vows when he'd said them. He'd hurt her because he hadn't trusted her to love Sara enough. He'd hurt her because he hadn't been able to admit what he felt for her. Lauren deserved a husband who could completely open his heart to her.

He could do that now.

But it might be too late. He loved Lauren in a way that he'd never loved before. It felt so deep and so breathtakingly true that he couldn't imagine his life or Sara's without her. But could she forgive him a second time? Would she let him prove his love for her?

When Eli pushed open the door to the examining room, Cody had made up his mind about what to do. "I need a favor."

"Anything," the older man said.

"I want you to take me to Macmillan's Garden Center."

"Cody, you need to go home and rest—"

"I can't rest. Not until I see Lauren. I've got to make this right."

After an appraising look Cody knew well, Eli agreed. "All right, I'll take you. Because if I don't I know you'll get there on your own steam despite the cost."

At her drafting board in the garden center's office, Lauren couldn't concentrate on much of anything. When the outside door opened and Rob came in, she cringed. He'd pretty much left her alone all day. But now, from the expression on his face, she knew he was going to grill her.

Still she tried to ignore him by picking up a pencil and shading in an area on her sketch.

"Are you ready to talk yet?" he asked from behind her right shoulder.

"There's nothing to talk about."

"You arrived at Mom and Dad's with your suitcase. You told them you'd be staying until you found an apartment. You wouldn't tell them anything else. You've hardly said a word to me all day. I think there's plenty to talk about.''

Turning to look at her brother, she said, "Maybe it's none of your business."

Undaunted he sat on the corner of his desk. "Maybe it's not. But I'm going to make it my business, because it's obvious you're miserable."

She couldn't deny that, and she knew Rob wasn't going to let this drop. So she told him the truth. "Cody doesn't love me. He as much as told me he'll never *let* himself love me."

After absorbing her words, Rob asked, "Does this have to do with his first marriage?"

Lauren simply nodded.

"I don't need details, Sis. But I want you to know I see a pattern here. You keep running away from Cody Granger."

"I don't..."

"You ran away from him that day you saw him kissing Gretchen when you were a teenager. You told me he wanted to take you to the prom but you wouldn't let him. Did you ever think that something good might have happened if you'd gone with him?"

"He loved Gretchen!"

"Did he? Maybe he didn't have anything to compare his relationship with Gretchen to. Maybe more would have developed between the two of you. But you didn't give it a chance."

She didn't need Rob making her feel worse. "I didn't *have* a chance," she retorted.

"Says you." After a long, pregnant moment, Rob challenged her again. "You ran away from Cody after your argument with him about Sara."

That night was forever etched in her memory. "I needed to think."

"Maybe. But you left. And now you've walked out again. What kind of message do you think that sends a man?"

"Whose side are you on?" she asked, hurt by his criticism.

"Yours."

Thinking about everything her brother had said, she realized how insecure she'd always felt around Cody. Is that why she kept running away? Did she think she wasn't good enough for him? Or was she simply scared to stand up for everything she felt for him?

She loved him so. Hadn't she shown him that every day since their marriage? Hadn't she proven her love? Couldn't he see it and feel it?

But you've never said it, a little voice scolded her. *And you* did *leave,* it went on, becoming louder.

She remembered the prom night he'd given her. What if Cody did have feelings for her? What if his pain from the past as well as his pride were just hiding them?

The outside door opened again. Expecting to see her mom or dad, Lauren was shocked to see Eli and Cody...even more shocked to see a bandage on Cody's jaw and arm, the torn jeans with white gauze peeking through on his leg, as well as a cane in his hand.

"What happened?" Lauren asked.

But Cody brushed the question away. "It's not important."

Apparently, Eli thought it was. "He took a spill on his bike and should be home in bed. But he's so damn stubborn he insisted I bring him here." Stepping outside once more, Eli added, "If either of you needs me, I'll be looking at the begonias."

Rob glanced from Cody to Lauren and then said, "I'll show Eli something more interesting than begonias. Yell if you need a referee."

Lauren barely heard either of them. She couldn't bear to think of Cody hurt. And he *was* hurt. That was too obvious. She longed to brush the lines of pain from his forehead. But she remained where she was.

"How did it happen?" she asked.

The play of emotions on Lauren's face gave Cody hope that she still cared, that he hadn't destroyed all of her feelings for him. He knew he didn't deserve a second chance. He didn't deserve this woman who'd married him to save his relationship with his daughter. And who, hopefully, had had other reasons, too.

"I was down by the creek and skidded. But that doesn't matter."

Moving deeper into the room, he leaned the cane against Rob's desk, wanting to reach out and take her into his arms. But he couldn't yet, and he just prayed he could find the words to make up for everything he'd said and done. "I've been an idiot, Lauren. I wanted to do everything right, and I've done everything wrong."

She studied him for a very long heartbeat before she responded softly, "I shouldn't have run away from you last night. That wasn't the way to show you…how much you mean to me. That wasn't the way to teach you how to believe in love again."

His heart pounding now, he took her face between

his hands, hoping he was reading her right, hoping she would believe what he had to say. "I *do* believe in love. I believe in *your* love. You've shown it to me in so many ways. I was a blind fool not to see it sooner. I was a fool not to realize how much I loved you—how much I love you."

Lauren's brown eyes widened in surprise, then brimmed with tears. "Oh, Cody. You really mean it? You're not just—"

"Saying it so we'll stay married? Saying it to protect my relationship with Sara?"

Lauren tried to turn away from him, but he wouldn't let her. "I have so much to make up to you for."

"You had a lot to deal with," she murmured, still not looking as if she believed him. "We went into marriage thinking it would be convenient, hoping it would work...."

Stroking her cheek, he shook his head. "You came to me with so much generosity of spirit, I should have been down on my knees thanking you. Instead, I was keeping a padlock on my heart, afraid to let you in."

He slid his hands into her hair, determined to convince her his love was real and would last. "You managed to get in, anyway, Lauren. I love you for so many reasons, I can't count them all. I love the way you make me laugh, I love the deep-brown of your eyes, and I love the sweetness of your smile. You're everything I've ever wanted, and if you give me another chance, I'll prove my love every day in as many ways as I can find. Will you be my wife? Will you let me love you for a lifetime?"

As tears rolled down her cheeks, the reality of his

love finally dawned in her brown eyes. When it did, she locked her arms around his neck. "Yes, I'll be your wife." Then she added, "And I promise I'll never run away from you again."

When Cody kissed Lauren, his whole world became brighter, lighter, full of the joy and promise he never thought he would know. Lauren's response promised him that they'd have the rest of their lives together to prove their love to each other.

When they finally leaned away to catch their breaths, Cody brushed lingering tears from her cheeks. "Sara's staying with Dolores tonight... maybe for a few days. I finally realized I was punishing Dolores for my disappointment with my marriage to Gretchen."

"It takes a courageous man to admit that," Lauren said.

"It takes a courageous woman to love a man who *has* to admit that."

She shook her head. "I don't need courage to love you, Cody. It's as natural as breathing."

Her words filled all the empty places inside him. He'd never done anything in his life to deserve a woman like this, and he would do everything in his power to make her happy. Drawing her up from her chair, he wrapped his arms around her. "Come home with me. I want to make love to you."

She tenderly touched the bandage on his jaw. "I think Eli prescribed bed rest."

Catching her hand, he smiled. "We'll *be* in bed. I just won't be resting." Nothing would keep him from making sweet, tender love to his wife tonight.

Her eyes locked on his, she teased with a sly smile,

"Since you're the doctor, I guess you know what you need."

His smile slipped away as he said solemnly, "I need you."

With their bodies pressed together, their hearts beat as one. When Cody kissed Lauren, he knew he would not only love her, but cherish her...until the end of time.

Epilogue

It was the end of June when Lauren and Cody walked hand in hand through the gardens she'd designed for the office complex in Denver. He'd encouraged her every step of the way. Today he'd made sure he wasn't on call so they could enjoy her accomplishment. Her parents and Kim, Rob, Lindsey and Matthew, as well as Dolores and Sara, had just left after celebrating her success with her. Dolores had offered to take Sara for the night so that Lauren and Cody could have some time alone.

Lauren watched Craig Davis approach her and Cody as they stood by a fountain surrounded by boxwood.

"You should be very proud of yourself," the architect told her. "I'm hearing one compliment after another. The sculpture garden in the courtyard is a big hit."

"Thanks, Craig." She glanced up at her husband. Cody draped his arm around her shoulders and gave her a squeeze. "I told you the reviews would be great." Cody's jealousy of Craig had vanished. Now that they were secure in each other's love, it seemed that they could move mountains together.

And not only move mountains, but...

As soon as they sat down to an intimate dinner alone tonight, she had something wonderful to tell Cody. She looked at her husband with all the love she felt for him.

Craig cleared his throat, then said, "I'm going to circulate. Lauren, give me a call when you're ready to submit your ideas for the new performing arts center."

After Craig strode away, Cody smiled. "I think you've arrived."

Her career was important, but suddenly she couldn't wait to tell him her news. She didn't need a quiet restaurant, a table for two or candlelight. Instead she took his hand and tugged him toward a small garden with a sundial and a park bench.

"Where are we going?" he asked, amused.

"I have something to tell you."

"And you think I should be sitting down for it?"

"Maybe." The tone of her voice caught his attention immediately.

"What is it?" He looked concerned.

"I saw Eli again. This time I went straight to him...to make sure..."

"To make sure of what?" There was a hopeful light in Cody's eyes.

She only kept him in suspense for a moment. "Sara is going to have a brother or sister."

Cody's face broke into a grin, and he swept her up into his arms. "For sure?"

"For sure. It's official. You're happy about it?"

"Do you have any doubt about that?"

There was so much love in his voice, so much love in his eyes, that she could never doubt it. Her life with Cody was a dream come true. Whenever he kissed her, the passion was new and exciting all over again. And when he made love to her, she felt like a cherished bride and knew she would be for the rest of her life.

"Let's go home now," she suggested.

He set her back on her feet but kept his arms around her. "Not everybody's finished congratulating you."

"I don't need their congratulations. I just need you holding me."

His arms tightened. "I'll hold you all night long."

Tipping up her chin, she asked, "Can we call Sara and tell her about the baby?"

"Sure. Or we can wait until Dolores brings her back home for dinner tomorrow."

"No, I'd like to tell her tonight."

Tenderly he stroked his fingers down the side of Lauren's face. "I hope you're not worrying. She'll love the idea of having a brother or sister."

"Can we ask Eli and Dolores to be the godparents?"

"Are you sure your family won't mind?"

"My family will act like godparents, regardless."

His smile returned. "Then that's an absolutely wonderful idea. I want Dolores to realize she'll always be part of our family. And with Eli taking her to concerts and the theater, who knows what will happen if we give them a little time."

To their delight Eli and Dolores had been dating

over the past month. Eli would be coming for dinner, too, tomorrow along with Lauren's parents and Kim and Rob.

"We're going to have a full house tomorrow with everyone there."

"I never knew what a full house was until I married you." Cody's words were tender and loving, and she knew he meant them.

"How many children do you want?" she asked softly.

"I think we'll let that up to Someone who knows better than we do." With his hands clasping hers, Cody pulled her to him and kissed her forehead. "Are you sure you want to leave?"

"Absolutely." And with the confidence she felt in their love, she stood on tiptoe and kissed him soundly. When his arms wrapped around her once more, she didn't care who looked on. Cody's love had made her confident and sure and complete.

She was his, and he was hers. Forever.

* * * * *

Look for Karen Rose Smith's
next Silhouette Romance,
TALL, DARK AND TRUE,
in March 2001!

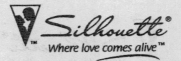

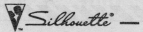